Oscillate

Susan M Higgins

SUSAN M HIGGINS

An Amazon paperback

First published in April 2019

ISBN number 9781091587007

Volume 2

Disclaimer

Oscillate is a work of fiction. Whilst places and areas are
factual, the characters, incidents and dialogue within this
book are purely fictional and are the products of the author's
imagination. Resemblances to individuals or events are
coincidental and are not to be construed as real.

HUMAN OSCILLATION

Human oscillation occurs daily. Back and forth we go, robotically saturated with unending routine.

Reluctant to change, we are scared to upset the balance.

When an unforeseen, negative event (or could it be a pre-determined event) abruptly confronts us, friction occurs and our equilibrium becomes over-stretched. Erratically, it moves backwards and forwards, struggling to regain its balance.

We enter a state of unsettled resistance and, steadfastly and unintentionally, we impede our natural flow.

We build walls. We suffer unnecessarily. Our bodies experience physical and psychological ills.

When we subconsciously clear out the past and forgive ourselves and others, instead of living in a cacophony of self-imposed disharmony, it is only then that our equilibrium will return.

Once we accept that a spiritual transition is ensuing and that the upheaval is taking us on the next step of our journey, we can move forward and our suffering ceases.

SUSAN M HIGGINS

AUTHOR'S NOTE

Human behaviour is complex.

Understanding human behaviour is even more complex; but understand it we should!

The rationales behind human behaviour are there to be explored and challenged.

Within this work of fiction, several aspects of the human psyche and the presence of spirit are explored; consideration being given as to how we can be 'of service' to each other as we journey throughout our lives.

Willingly, I invite you to interpret the novel and apply your rational discernment when critiquing the themes that I have, intentionally, chosen for inclusion.

PROLOGUE

She, an established author and highly-evolved individual, invites others to step into her personal sanctuary to allow them to heal.

Patiently, she watches as events unfold around her, intuitively aware that everyone in the group was meant to meet at this incredible moment in time.

****

He, an acclaimed abstract sculptor with a desire to release himself from his self-imposed guilt, uses introspective techniques to escape from his own personal prison.

Whilst doing so, he is given the opportunity to become the father that he always thought he would never be.

****

She, a sought-after interior designer, eventually finds the courage to unlock the padlocks from her imaginary, metal box and allow the controlling cobwebs of her past to escape freely into the ether. Serendipity calls on her and tenderly strokes her troubled mind.

He, a village doctor with an interest in alternative medicine, does not foresee the adventure that awaits him. His buried emotions surface and he makes decisions which will change his life.

****

He, an autistic young man who has recently lost his mother to Parkinson's Disease, is comforted and looked after by his close neighbours. Bereft and angry, he channels his heartache and his own experiences into helping others. Happiness awaits him.

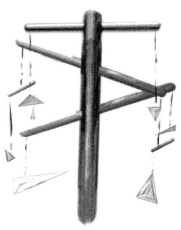

I would like to express my sincere thanks to Steve, Maureen, Sue, Linda and Carmel for taking the time to proofread and critique this novel.

Special thanks also to Heather, who was instrumental in the illustration and design of the amazing images and book cover.

All of your efforts are very much appreciated.

OSCILLATE

To and fro
Back and forth
Ebb and flow

Human oscillation
Perpetual routines
Reluctance to shift

Unforeseen friction
Sanity provoked
Forcing imperative change

Indecisive, unsettled
Undulating, erratic
Resisting the flow

Impromptu awakening
Recognition takes place
Transition unfolds

Freedom is felt
Equilibrium intact
Oscillation restored

To and fro
Back and forth
Ebb and flow

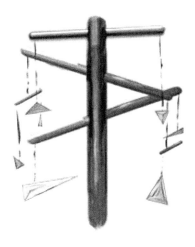

CHAPTER ONE

Slipping off her sandals, she stepped over the narrow, pebble-lined stream onto a paved area. The predictable Mediterranean sun had already reached 28° and it was only 11.00 am. It was going to be another 'hot one'. As she gazed into the transparent, trickling water it quietly soothed her unsettled thoughts.

Allowing her troubled mind to stray, she meandered along the curves of the long, winding path, before stopping for a moment to take in the fragrance of the wildflowers and the aromatic herbs; all living organically and harmoniously alongside several types of fruit trees on either side of the path.

She brushed her hands over the tops of some lavender foliage and plucked a few sprigs. Crushing them in the palms of her warm hands, the evocative smell wafted through the air, imparting a calming sensation as it reached her nostrils. The scent held special memories for her. Nearly twelve months to the day, she had created her own wedding bouquet and buttonholes out of the sprigs from this very same plant.

As she continued on her stroll, the clearing within the orchard came into sight. On reaching her destination she began to feel better. This place was her peaceful haven; her sanctuary.

An intricate, triangular labyrinth with a central, triangular sculpture welcomed her. A steady flow of water emerged from the top of the sculpture and cascade down each side into a moat-like channel. Labyrinths are usually circular in design, but he knew that she had a penchant for all things triangular when he had designed and created it, especially for her.

To the left of her, under the shade of some fig trees, was a wooden summer house. Open-plan in design, it contained a spacious bench covered in bottle-green, checked cushions. Resting on a small table, in the centre of the summer house, was a lantern and some ceramic tea-light holders. A tall, symmetrical, amethyst geode stood in a corner, providing spiritual protection.

She cast her mind back to the first time she had laid eyes on this mystical place. It was on the morning of her wedding. He had led her along the meditation path, before surprising her with the labyrinth. For weeks before the wedding her fiancé had given her strict orders. She should not to enter the clearing. If she needed any fruit or herbs for cooking, then he would gather them for her. He had laboured, solidly and singly, designing and creating this special place for her as a wedding gift.

Standing to the right of the labyrinth, in its own space, was a Calder-inspired, two metre high sculpture. The bold-coloured, triangular mobiles of red, yellow and white floated naturally and swirled involuntarily in the billowing breeze. The steel sculpture had been her wedding gift to him. She also had toiled for several weeks, designing and producing numerous maquettes, before engaging a local engineering company to build it and erect it. Her husband had named it Oscillate. He felt that the harmonic movements represented the ebb and flow of human life and nature.

Suzette and her husband were two highly-creative, introspective individuals. Independent and yet intuitively aware of their interdependence on each other, they were sensitive to each other's spiritual energy and needs.

Serge was a sculptor, renowned for his many works of abstract art; most of which had been displayed in several galleries during the last forty years. Some of his larger pieces had graced the foyers of large corporates throughout France; others had been shipped over to America. His father, was also a celebrated artist and sculptor. He had taught Serge many vital skills, nurturing refinement of his techniques.

Suzette Couture was an established author. Her simplistic and soul-searching novels, each with their spiritual 'food for thought' connotations, had inspired many of her readers to discover their own spiritual gifts and make positive enhancements within their own lives.

As an artist, her fascination with geometric and figurative abstraction, had featured in many pieces of her non-objective art.

She walked over to the labyrinth and took her position at the entrance. Preparing herself for the inward journey to the centre, she took several deep breaths. After stating her spiritual intention, she stepped onto the brightly-coloured, mosaic path. The coolness of the smooth marble beneath her bare feet sent a pleasant stream of sensations through her soles. Walking back and forth along the straight lines, she became lost in the moment; oblivious of any sound around her.

On reaching the centre she sat down, cross-legged and prepared herself for her meditation. Breathing slowly and deeply several times, she adjusted her posture before concentrating on connecting with her intention. Sitting still and upright, she closed her eyes, letting go of the many distracting thoughts that were so determined to infiltrate her subconscious. Relaxing her jaw and shoulders, she saw clouds of purple and green swirling behind her closed eyelids and she could feel herself starting to unwind.

Entering the silence, she gently drifted back to the intention she had stated at the entrance to the labyrinth. Her hands and feet were cold and a shiver ran down her spine. It felt as if someone was standing behind her, guiding her.

Concentrating on her heart chakra in the centre of her chest, she thought of Serge and his current state of health. Her channels now open, she focused; inhaling and exhaling deeply, she sent waves of positive energy to the man she dearly loved. A feeling of warmth embraced her. It was as if she was being wrapped up in cotton wool. A vibrating sensation pulsed inside her ears as she pictured a bright, white light surrounding him. She visualised him being released from the intense emotional pain which was suffocating him.

"Please help him, Lord. Please heal him", she prayed.

In her mind's eye she could see the sadness, in the form of murky, grey clouds, flowing out of his body and into the ether. Taking several deep breaths, she brought herself back and opened her eyes. Feeling a little shaky and light-headed, she rested for a moment. Emotional, she let her tears flow.

"Thank you", she whispered.

Standing up slowly, she again focused on

her breathing before commencing her outward journey. When she had entered the labyrinth, her body had intuitively informed her that she was out of balance. Returning to the entrance she felt more energised and calmer.

CHAPTER TWO

After completing her daily meditation session, Suzette called into the studio to see Serge. He'd been in one of his quiet phases, fixating totally on his work. As an artist herself, Suzette totally respected and understood his need for solitude; she too needed alone-time.

"Hello darling. Are you hungry? I'm going to prepare some lunch."

Serge was in the process of transforming a large piece of white marble into a sculpture. Five days ago, he had taken a one hour's drive to a mountainside quarry in Montpellier to carefully select the slab. Delivered two days later, he had spent much of his time since then making notes and surveying the marble before taking his chisel to it.

He'd been recently commissioned by a large corporate in Northern France to design and create a contemporary sculpture, depicting an aspect of their manufacturing process. Several drawings and maquettes later, he'd chalked the outline onto the four sides of the block and started pitching large chunks off the marble; eliminating the areas that weren't needed. His adept, innate ability to conceptualise how to get the best out of a slab of marble, was just one of the many talents that Suzette admired.

Acknowledging her presence, he placed his pointed chisel and mallet on his workbench, before removing his goggles and safety gloves.

"Bonjour, ma chérie. Oui. I am hungry. What shall we eat?"

"I've already prepared a mixed salad. Then I thought we could have some grilled salmon with a ginger and lime dressing. There's also some fresh carrots and beans that I gathered from the garden this morning."

"Délicieux."

As he walked towards her he winced, as the shooting pain in his back caught him unawares. The pain was always there, but lately it had become more persistent, limiting his ability to function fully on a day to day basis. His ultimate fear was that the pain may, one day, result in impairment and he wouldn't be able to walk, or even worse, practice his skills. It was unthinkable! He leant on his workbench for some support. The agony was unbearable.

Suzette went over to him and immediately placed her hands over his coccyx. Sensing the main area of his pain, she became aware of discomfort radiating up his spine and across his right shoulder. Moving her hands slowly over his body, she channelled her energy into the affected parts.

Serge yelped as a rush of heat penetrated his muscles, giving him some temporary relief.

"Hey, Suzette, I felt that!" Whatever you did to me though, it has taken some of the pain away."

He attempted to straighten up as best as he could. Although he was still leaning over to one side and slightly hunched, he pulled her towards him and held her close.

"Ma chérie, je t'aime", he whispered.

"I know you love me, Serge. Come on now, let's eat."

He interlocked his fingers into hers and they slowly walked back to the house.

Over lunch they discussed the results of his recent x-rays and MRI scan. The tests hadn't revealed any structural damage and the consultant had 'loosely' diagnosed muscle spasm. Following several visits to a chiropractor he'd been advised that it was 'wear and tear' relating to the nature of his job and that he may just have to learn to live with the pain. Although, he strongly advised that it would be beneficial if Serge attended for weekly treatment to ease the pain!

Suzette cut into the grilled salmon. Her knife sliced easily through the tender, juicy fillet. She placed a chunk into her mouth and the flakes melted on her tongue. The ginger had a kick to it and the lime dressing felt tangy and fresh.

After finishing her meal, she placed her knife and fork in a straight line in the centre of her plate and waited for Serge to finish eating before she spoke.

"I know you don't want to hear this again, Serge. Even though I think the massage may help you temporarily, I don't honestly believe that it will get to the root of your problem."

Serge raised his eyebrows. He knew what she was saying and he knew that she was right. He was aware of his unconscious, emotional issues and was still reluctant to face up to them. It was too painful to re-live them; even worse than the physical pain he already endured.

Suzette knew only too well, through her own experiences and those of the people who had attended her courses, that the lingering pain within the soul is, almost always, manifested through various types of chronic, physical pain in different parts of the body. She had discussed this with him several times and, whilst he agreed with her, he always managed to put it to the back of his mind.

She also knew that the build-up of negative energy which he had attempted to suppress for so long was affecting his equilibrium.

As if on cue, the excruciating pain returned, startling him and taking his breath away.

"Ouch. I know exactly what you're thinking, Suzette. You are right in what you say. I know you are, but I am too scared to go there."

She understood his fears and she wouldn't force him. It was ultimately his decision. She could not live his life for him, nor did she want to. He would have to work through it himself.

"Serge, you'll know when you are ready. Your mind and your body and your soul will let you know."

He knew that it was only a matter of time. Francesca, his deceased first wife, had been telling him for a while now on her regular visits to him.

Unbeknown to Serge, Francesca had also visited Suzette!

CHAPTER THREE

Suzette was busy pottering in the garden, mulching round the plants and watering them. Interestingly, before coming to live in France she hadn't been much of a gardener and yet, here in the wonderful wilderness of Villa d'Couture Atelier, she'd gained immense pleasure out of growing and eating her own organic food. Understanding the transience of life, gardening had made her even more mindful of nature. She counted her blessings for everything she had. As well as keeping her fit, gardening was therapeutic; it fed her soul as well as her body.

The phone rang again. It hadn't stopped

ringing all morning. By the time she got to it she knew that it would stop. It did! The answer machine flashed with a message and she pressed the 'play' button.

"Hi, Suzette. Just ringing to see where you are up to with your chapters. Can we work on a deadline of four weeks for submitting the first draft? Give me a call when you get this message. Speak soon. Bye."

Her publisher had been pushing her to complete her fourth novel for the last three months. Due to having other things on her mind, she'd been struggling to concentrate. Writer's block was the last thing she needed now. She knew she had to complete it and would email them later.

Instead of returning to her gardening, she called in the studio to see Serge. After yesterday's occurrence, she wanted to check on him. She found him chipping away at the slab. With careful precision, the mallet struck the pitching tool and the force of his powerful hit shattered the marble. She admired his rhythmic style when he was 'roughing out' the slab. *Chip chip, chip chip, chip chip.* Intrigued, she seriously considered that the hammering sound itself could be deemed as a work of art.

His physique hadn't changed that much since when she first saw him over three years ago. His hair now had more silver in it, but was still collar-length. His muscular arms, his hairy chest, toned thighs and calves still excited her. Holidaying at the time in Olvano, she'd been taking her morning stroll along the banks of the Canal du Midi, when she first set eyes on him. His garden backed onto the canal and, most mornings, she saw him chipping away at his sculptures. She had made a point of practising her limited knowledge of the French language, calling out 'Bonjour Monsieur.' He would sometimes acknowledge her with a civil 'Bonjour Madame', but didn't attempt further conversation; which had disappointed her somewhat. Neither did he smile. Sometimes, he just nodded his head.

It was only the following year, when she'd moved to France permanently, that she had met up with him again. She'd been shopping for fabric at Lezignan market and had called into a bar for a cool beer. The weather had been scorching hot. He'd been sitting there and they'd made a connection. It had been meant to happen and, when he invited her to his home to drink champagne, she took him up on his offer. Ten months after the encounter she'd married him. He'd unexpectedly proposed to her one morning after they'd just made love.

Suzette, although happy just to live with him, had accepted his offer. She loved him. She had waited several lifetimes to be re-united with him. It was the right thing to do. Suzette Stark became Madame Couture.

The many commonalities they shared were implausible to others, but not to Suzette and Serge.

Knowing each other internally, they sensed each other's thoughts and feelings. They were a perfect fit in many ways.

Intuitively aware of her presence – he had sensed her arrival but didn't speak – he stopped chipping. Removing his goggles and ear-muffs he beckoned her.

"Bonjour, ma chérie". Come and look."

She walked over to him and kissed his lips.

"Tell me, darling. Are you making good progress?"

He nodded.

"I've almost completed the general shape of it. I need to make a few more measurements and then I'll use my claw chisel to create some parallel lines. I'll need to mark out again and then I'll use a much shallower stroke to add some more texture. It needs to fit into an industrial setting so a smooth finish to the sculpture wouldn't really suit. Texture is fundamental to this specific piece. I want it to be tactile and thought-provoking."

His energetic approach to the way he worked fascinated Suzette. She'd previously used similar techniques, although on a much smaller scale, when she'd carved an entwined, male and female figure out of a solid, dense building block. It had been a slow, satisfying process but she had thoroughly enjoyed creating it.

"I've been watching you work and you inspire me. In fact, I'm awestruck."

He chuckled. "Are you darling?" He leant

over and kissed her.

"The way you use your tools is like listening to music. You have such rhythm in the way you work. I could watch you all day. I wish I could work with a large slab like you do. I've only worked on small pieces", she admitted.

"I'll teach you one day. Maybe when I have completed this one, we can work on some fresh ideas together. Maybe we could have our own exhibition in our atelier!"

"I would love that." Would you like to walk the labyrinth with me? I think you're in need of a break."

He nodded. Even though he knew he had a deadline to reach, he knew also that he should listen to his body – and to his wife! He removed his overalls.

She nestled into him as he placed his arm around her shoulders and guided her across the stream. She was aroused by the freshness of his body odour and the sensual undertones of his memorable cologne - *Eau Savage*. Quintessentially French, like her handsome husband, she loved the stimulating smell of the lemony and woody undertones. He'd always used this cologne and it suited his personality.

In silence, they walked the meditation path until they reached the clearing.

"Let's sit awhile in the summer house, Suzette. My back aches."

Without speaking they reflected, focusing

their attention on the trickling sounds from the water sculpture and were mesmerized by the colourful, triangular mobiles oscillating effortlessly in the gentle breeze. Cultivating the silent echoes within their own tranquil space, they meditated; Serge concentrating on eliminating his internal chatter and Suzette praying that he would find inner peace.

Fifteen minutes later Suzette navigated her way around the labyrinth and contemplated on her intention, whilst Serge remained in the summer house.

Her meditation completed, she leisurely followed the path back to the entrance of the labyrinth to where Serge waiting for her.

"Do you feel a little better now, Serge?"

"Yes, I do. My mind seems a bit clearer and the pain in my back has eased slightly."

After making their way back to the house, they prepared lunch together and carried it on trays to the pool area. Munching on *Salade Verte* and slices of grilled tofu with a sun-dried tomato dressing, they toasted their health with glasses of sparkling Limoux.

The temperature had reached a staggering 35° and it was forecast to reach 38° by the late afternoon.

Stripping off their clothes, they swam naked in the coolness of the pool before returning to their sun-loungers to dry off in the afternoon sun.

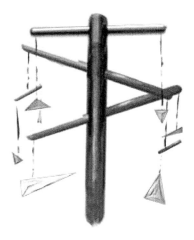

CHAPTER FOUR

It was their first wedding anniversary. They were going to celebrate it by driving along the coast to Collioure and whilst they were there, they would meet up with Serge's friend, Gabriel Le-Tissier, who was a doctor with his own general practice in a nearby village.

They knew the roads would be busy and that Collioure would be heaving with tourists - it was middle of July after all – but they loved the artisan quarter and the village was so romantic.

When they'd first met they had visited the 'City of Painters' and had paid many more visits since then. Ambling through the bustling streets of Collioure, people-watching, gave Suzette ideas for her writing. Maybe she would be inspired today; her publishers had called yet again to confirm the deadline.

Serge looked at her and smiled.

Happy anniversary, ma chérie."

"Happy anniversary to you too, Serge. We'd better get up and have breakfast. We have a busy day ahead of us."

He raised his eyebrows and kissed her. "I thought we'd just had our breakfast." His spontaneous, dry sense of humour resonated with her own similar, sharp wit.

Whilst Suzette showered, Serge walked over to the local patisserie. When he returned, Suzette was in the garden plucking some fresh peppermint. Neither of them drank tea or coffee. Instead they used herbs from their garden and infused them to make a refreshing drink. The smell of the peppermint was equally as refreshing as its taste and it was good for the digestion.

They set the table together. Laden heavily with crusty French baguettes, croissants au beurre, pan au chocolat, apricot and lavender confiture, creamy fromage frais and blueberries, they sampled everything.

"Who would believe we've been married for one whole year. It has passed so quickly", said Suzette as she spread a large helping of her home-made confiture onto a thick chunk of baguette.

The intense, sharpness of the apricots (she'd used only a small amount of sugar) and the subtle flavour of the lavender tickled her taste buds and she licked her lips.

Her neighbour had advised her to use a tiny sprig of lavender in the confiture, to discourage mould forming on the soft fruit. It had worked.

"It has, but I do feel as if I've known you forever", Serge responded as he broke a large chunk off a croissant.

"Maybe you have", she intuitively replied.

He smiled knowingly. He really appreciated every moment of his life with her. He was grateful for every day that he shared with her.

Suzette cleared the breakfast table whilst Serge rushed upstairs to shower and change his clothes.

It was yet another glorious day and the temperature already 22°. She'd decided to wear one of her multi-coloured, shift dresses, sewn from a length of linen she'd bought at Lezignan market. She'd sewn a scarf out of left-over fabric and she used it as a hair band to keep her hair off her face. Maybe it was time to get it cut. It would be so much cooler in the hot climate, but Serge liked her hair longer. A quick flick of mascara and a lavish smearing of fuschia lipstick and she was ready. Having already slathered herself in factor 30 sunscreen, she placed the bottle in her bag; ready to top up if needed later in the day. It would get hotter; the weather had been forecast as reaching up to 35° again.

She wasn't complaining. The charm of French country life really suited Suzette. The sun's healing powers provided her with a generous dose of vitamin D and it boosted her serotonin levels. For most of her life she'd lived in the North West of England where it always seemed to be raining. Lanquedoc had been quoted as having up to three hundred days of sunshine per year and she was more than content living in the region.

They made their way towards Perpignan, travelling along the Costal D81 through Canet-Plage, St Cyprian-Plage and Argeles, until they reached Collioure just before noon. They had arranged to meet Gabriel at 1.00pm, so they strolled around the port and mingled with the tourists in the narrow streets. Chatting with the resident artists, they discreetly critiqued their work before making their way back to *Les Templiers Restaurant*; more commonly known as the 'Open Window of Collioure'. They'd visited this eccentric restaurant on many previous occasions. Suzette had researched the history of the area and was quite surprised to discover that Les Templiers was first opened in 1895. She also liked the idea that Picasso, Matisse, Dali and Duffy had frequented the place, paying for their food and drink with some of their paintings.

Gabriel was already there waiting for them to arrive. He'd secured a table for them on the covered patio area. After their arrival, they chatted whilst glancing at the multi-coloured boats bobbing up and down in the harbour and the countless tourists strolling along the pathway in front of the restaurant.

An aromatic *melange* of appetising cuisine permeated Suzette's nostrils. She was tempted to have fish for starters, but she decided on chickpea and lime marinated mushrooms. She chose poached lobster chunks with sun-dried tomatoes and lemongrass dressing for her main dish. Gabriel ordered an artichoke, fig and parmesan salad and pan-seared lemon trout almondine, whilst Serge stuck to his usual lunchtime starter – a warm goat's cheese salad. He ordered pan-seared sea scallops with cauliflower puree and fried capers for his main course.

The food arrived, artistically arranged on white platters and they all tucked in with relish. Between mouthfuls, Serge imparted his symptoms to Gabriel and informed him of how the tests on his back had not revealed any damage. Gabriel listened intently and nodded. He had seen patients who had displayed Serge's symptoms on several occasions. They also had undergone many tests to eliminate spinal or structural damage and their tests had also been inconclusive. As he wasn't Serge's own general practitioner, he couldn't professionally diagnose him, but as a close friend, he could advise him. He told Serge that he believed that the back pain he was experiencing could be Tension Myositis Syndrome, (TMS).

Suzette had heard of this syndrome before. Two separate clients who had attended her self-development courses had been diagnosed with TMS. She'd always suspected that her husband's back problem could be a physical response to a psychological process; namely his ex-wife's lengthy illness, culminating in her passing.

Interested in Gabriel's prognosis, Serge remained silent whilst Gabriel continued to explain.

"At the time of diagnosis and during the treatment of Francesca's cancer and the traumatic closing stages of her life, you were psychologically overwhelmed, Serge. Your mind unconsciously protected you by blocking out your emotions, because they were much too painful for you to deal with."

Serge nodded his head several times. "At times my head and my heart felt as if they were going to burst, but I had to keep going and be strong for her. I couldn't let her see my pain. She was in enough pain herself."

"I can remember speaking to you several times during her illness and her ongoing chemotherapy treatment. You said that you were coping when, in fact, you weren't. Your body was taking all the strain. You continued to put extra pressure on yourself by not asking for help. You wanted to do everything for Francesca and the internal demands you put yourself under were extremely intense. You suffered the consequences of your actions and you're still suffering now."

Serge bowed his head and tried to control his tears. Suzette reached for his hand and held it firmly. She handed him a tissue.

Gabriel continued to converse in a formal doctor's tone. "Back pain is difficult to diagnose, Serge. Sometimes the causes show up on x-rays and scans and sometimes tests prove inconclusive – as in your case."

"Yes, that's what the specialist told me. I couldn't understand it. Undeniably, I thought I was going insane, when I definitely knew that the pain was there. Sometimes, when I bend down, I can't straighten up fully."

"You are holding all of your sorrow and resentment in your back. The trauma, which you endured for so long, eventually manifested itself in your chronic back pain."

Serge sat upright in his chair, altering his poise. "The pain is not just at the bottom of my spine, it moves around from side to side and goes up to my shoulder blades. I also get a tingling sensation and a feeling of numbness in my hands. I initially thought that the numbness may be an occupational hazard."

Suzette squeezed his hand to reassure him. She was concerned by the lengthy endurance of his suffering and the harm it was causing him.

"What you have described is all related to psychogenic musculoskeletal and nerve symptoms. I agree, the numbness and tingling could possibly be due to repetitive strain injury, when you are hammering away at your sculptures, but as I have said before, I feel certain that it is psychologically related."

Feeling relieved that it was nothing sinister, even though the consultants had already reassured him otherwise, Serge questioned Gabriel further.

"What do you think I can I do about it, Gabriel? I'm getting desperate now. It really is affecting my quality of life."

"Well, Serge. I'm speaking off the record here, because I'm not your GP and some older members of the medical community still do not accept TMS as a condition, also known as the Mind Body Syndrome. However, in offering you my professional opinion, I do think that this is what you are experiencing."

Suzette nodded. She had been waiting for an opportunity to speak and addressed Gabriel.

"Serge and I have spoken several times about his symptoms. He knows what he must do. He must clear his past issues and deal with them in a rational way. Ten years ago, I devised a self-actualisation programme. I have delivered it many times to small groups and individuals, with much success. It can be a painful process but it works. I have used the same method with a GP in England who had experienced several traumas in his life. He now uses my alternative principles to treat many of his patients instead of prescribing drugs."

Gabriel listened intently as Suzette outlined the elements of the programme. He wondered whether she'd adopted some of Carl Jung's theories when she'd designed and developed it.

"Have you heard of Carl Gustav Jung, Suzette?"

Suzette smiled.

"I have. I've studied several of his books and I'm in total agreement with his theories. I have always believed that the mind and body work together and that the mind has an incredible ability to heal the body. With respect, I know you are a doctor and your views may be scientific, so you may choose to disagree with me. However, I have witnessed many occasions where the mind has healed the body."

Gabriel rested his hand on his chin and pondered before answering.

"On the contrary, Suzette. I do agree with your statement. I also greatly admire and respect Jung's theories and his principles. I studied his philosophies in medical school. In fact one of my theoretical dissertations was based on Carl Jung. Writing it enlightened me to the fact that I should not discard the spiritual aspects of life. I would love to know more about what you do. In the meantime, Serge, I think you would benefit greatly from your wife's experience. Let her help you."

Suzette, delighted to discover that she had some commonality with Gabriel, immediately offered him an invitation.

"Come to dinner next Saturday evening, Gabriel. We can talk more. I'm so glad we met up with you today. Is seven okay for you?"

Thoughts swirling around his head, Serge pondered on the conversation and he wondered whether the diagnosis could be correct. If it was, then there was some hope. All he had to do was get his head around facing past issues. He needed to get rid of the tormented feelings. Maybe the opening of old wounds would eventually bring him some peace and heal his back pain.

Adopting a more informal tone, Gabriel accepted. "Seven is great for me, Suzette. I look forward to it."

He walked around to where Serge was sitting. "Have I been of help, my friend?

Serge got up from his chair. "You have given me much 'food for thought', Gabriel. I will digest what you have said and I promise you that I'll act on it. Merci, mon ami."

Gabriel held Serge close for a while and kissed him on both cheeks. The warmth that Serge shared with his close friends touched Suzette. She really admired the way that French men were not afraid to embrace and be tactile with each other. Her only experiences of English men hugging and kissing in this way, were when goals had been scored on the football pitch!

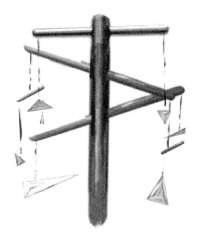

CHAPTER FIVE

He woke up sweating profusely. It was 4.00am. His recurring dreams were now becoming more frequent. In his dream he had to get to the other side of a raging, murky river to rescue Francesca. Each time he tried to cross it, the torrents got stronger and he had to wait for the water to slow down before he could even attempt it. She was calling out his name, begging him for help and he couldn't reach her. He was shouting to her, telling her that he was coming to her but she kept fading into the distance; the wind blowing her away until he could see her no more. His shouting woke him up every time, as it did this time, accompanied by an intense pain in his lower back.

He lay motionless by Suzette's side. Thank God, she hadn't heard him. She was sleeping soundly and he didn't want to wake her; or could it be he'd only been shouting in his subconscious? He knew his dreams were trying to communicate important messages. Examining the contents, he tried to understand the meaning behind them.

Serge related the raging river to his own anger and self-doubt; his challenge of crossing the river being more difficult than he'd imagined it to be. He correlated the crossing of the river to a transition in his life – deducing that it needed to be crossed in order to move on with his life after Francesca's death; to stop feeling he was somehow to blame for her death and to trust that he could defeat his feelings of guilt, if he put his mind to it.

He thought of the stream in his garden and how he had to cross it to reach the labyrinth, where healing could take place; his reasoning being, that it was necessary to cross the stream so he could enjoy a peaceful future with Suzette. Maybe, subconsciously, that had been why he'd been inspired to build the meditation path and labyrinth, especially for her.

On a more positive note, he associated the raging torrents and the wind with impending, rapid change. Instead of procrastinating, like he'd done for the past couple of years, he realised that it was time to clear the past and move on with his life.

Suzette hadn't heard him shouting but had sensed his restlessness. She turned over and faced him.

"What's the matter, Serge?" Are you having trouble sleeping?"

"I keep having the same dream, over and over again and every time, it wakes me up. Did you hear me shouting?"

"No. I didn't hear you, but I knew that you were awake." She snuggled into him.

He relayed the contents of his dream to her and his assumptions. From her own experience, she was aware that dreams could reveal so much more than they mask. She was also conscious that individuation was occurring, especially when Serge had explained how he'd connected his dreams to his waking life and how he'd tried to process the true meaning of them.

"Suzette, do you think that my dreams are the embodiment of my thoughts and my repressed feelings?"

"I think that your dreams are encouraging you to resolve your inner struggles."

"I think I'm ready now. No, I *know* I am ready to start the clearing process."

She too knew that he was ready. He had reached a point where he had to face his issues.

"Let's talk about it in the morning. Try to get some sleep."

His head was spinning with his irrational thoughts. He was tired, but he didn't know if sleep would transpire.

Suzette got out of the bed and slotted a meditation CD in the player. She lit two tea-lights and placed a piece of amethyst under his pillow.

As the shadows danced around the candle-lit room, they lay in each other's arms waiting for the soothing music to lull them back into a deep sleep.

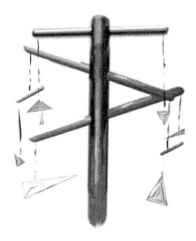

CHAPTER SIX

Over breakfast they discussed Serge's recurring dreams. His imperative urgency to validate the symbolic meanings of his recurring dreams and their significance, dominated the conversation. His own interpretation was that they were a natural manifestation of his subconscious mind, due to the nurturing of his 'perceived' guilt since the start of Francesca's illness.

"I am ready to clear, Suzette."

"Ok. Well, we could commence the process immediately if you want to. We can skip some of the initial processes because you're already in touch with your inner self; you know who you are and why you are here on this earth."

"Do you really think I am ready?

"I know you're ready, darling. However, introspection is intensive and can be emotionally challenging. You'll feel extremely tired as you work through your issues."

He sighed. "Gabriel is coming this evening. Maybe I should leave it until tomorrow. I am not trying to put if off though", he added honestly.

Suzette agreed.

"I think that's a good idea. You don't want to appear rude, if your mind is focused on your clearing process. Anyhow, I must prepare the food for this evening, so that'll take up most of my time today."

Serge cleared the breakfast table, whilst she set about preparing the food. They had already decided on the dinner menu the evening before. For starters, they'd have individual Gruyere cheese and chive soufflés. For the main course, she would bake lime and garlic trout and roast some fresh vegetables and herbs, from their own garden, with sprinklings of balsamic vinegar and chilli flakes. The dessert, a favourite of hers, would be lemon and ginger syllabub, garnished with organic, dark-chocolate shavings.

Her love of cooking had returned since she had met Serge. When she'd lived on her own, she had cooked simple, healthy meals but hadn't made that much of an effort to cook special meals for herself.

She prepared the main dish first. Using a food processor, she combined the flesh, juice and zest of two limes with two tablespoons of creamed garlic, oil and parsley. She arranged the fillets of trout into three foil parcels and poured the mixture over them, before putting them in the fridge to marinate. The zest of the lime and the sweet, pungent ginger would slowly seep into the fish ready for cooking later.

As she whipped the cream and the sugar together for the syllabub, she thought of what Gabriel had said. She hadn't expected him to take an interest in alternative therapies and was looking forward to conversing with him this evening.

Once the peaks had formed on the cream, she gently folded the blend of ginger wine, lemon rind and lemon juice – which had been gradually infusing since the day before - into the mixture and added tiny pieces of crystallised ginger. After piling the syllabub into three tall tumblers, she placed them into the fridge. Suzette would garnish them later.

Wanting the soufflés to be just perfect, she wouldn't attempt to make the mixture until about 6.00pm.

Feeling a little peckish, she snacked on a few medijool dates and a handful of walnuts before walking around to the studio to see if Serge was ready to eat lunch.

She found him, deep in thought, pacing slowly and deliberately around his masterpiece; examining it from different angles.

"Is it nearly finished, Serge?"

"I am nearing the final stage. Some parts I will leave rough. Others will need smoothing off. Smoothing off can be such a tedious process but it is a very worthwhile one. The procedure will accentuate the patterns in the marble and it will give it a magnificent, translucent sheen. I'll make a decision whether to use a tin or iron oxide after I've finished sanding it."

In awe of his talent, Suzette admired the way in which he'd carefully surveyed the site and collaborated with the organisation's CEO before exploring how his piece of work would fit into the specific setting within the enormous entrance area.

Serge had been sensitively concerned with the nature of the space that his sculpture would inhabit; and equally as important, the statement it would make in relation to the company's ethos.

"I have a strict deadline to meet. I'll need to work solidly on the sculpture for the next few days, if I'm to complete it in good time. The transporters will come to collect it next Thursday; although the sculpture won't be unveiled until ten days later."

Suzette innately knew that when he had finally handed over the sculpture to the buyer, he would be left with a bitter-sweet feeling of loss and achievement. He'd nurtured an incredibly intimate relationship with this metamorphic piece of rock and he would be reluctant to let it go. She also knew that he would experience a deep sense of satisfaction, knowing that his work would be displayed in an area where it would be viewed and admired by many.

The sculpture was heavy enough and had been sensibly designed in such a way that it would be balanced adequately, to eliminate the need for a mounting block. It would be placed directly onto the marble floor, in the exact place which had been agreed on.

He removed the gloves from his sweaty and sore hands. One of the disadvantages of working with marble is that it absorbs the oil from the skin when it is touched and, whilst Serge loved to feel the marble, he wanted his work to be flawless; hence the wearing of the finely-woven gloves.

Although tactile and three dimensional in appearance, he was concerned that if viewers were allowed to handle the sculpture, the texture of his work would be altered. He'd already discussed this aspect with the CEO. It would be his decision if he allowed viewers to touch it. Once Serge had finally handed over his masterpiece at the unveiling ceremony and, the remainder of the fee was in his bank, it would no longer belong to him.

"I also have a deadline to reach, Serge. The publishers are pushing me for the final chapters. The proof-readers and my editors have a stringent deadline to work towards and my new novel needs completing; soon!"

"Are you hungry, Suzette? I am."

As they walked back to the house, hand in hand, they discussed future projects.

He'd spoken many times of working with different and unlikely media and, although he would always have a leaning towards abstraction, he was willing to explore new avenues.

"Maybe, we can work together on a piece of art, Suzette."

"I look forward to that, Serge. We can influence each other."

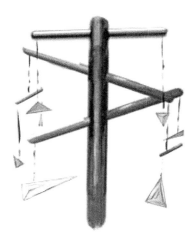

CHAPTER SEVEN

Gabriel was prompt. At precisely seven o'clock a loud knock on the door signalled his arrival.

The taxi was turning around in the driveway as Suzette and Serge opened the door. Gabriel was carrying a box and he placed it on a side table before hugging and kissing them both.

He'd brought with him a case of six bottles of 1531 Blanquette de Limoux for Suzette. He knew that she liked the aromatic crispness of this particular wine and would appreciate his gesture.

"Bonsoir Suzette. Bonsoir Serge. Ca va?"

"Bonsoir Gabriel. Je vais bien merci", they

both replied in unison.

"I selected this wine especially for you, Suzette.

"Merci beaucoup". It's a favourite of mine, as you can see."

She handed Gabriel and Serge a glass of ice-cold Limoux and left them chatting whilst she went to check on the soufflés.

She was pleased that Serge's friends had supported him throughout his traumatic period. Gabriel, Guy, Gaston and Thierry had attended school with Serge and they had remained friends throughout their adult lives. Although Suzette had many acquaintances in England, there were only a handful of people that she called her friends. She had always been a loner of sorts; by choice. When she'd first holidayed in Olvano, several years ago, the ex-pats and several villagers had nicknamed her 'The English Recluse'.

"Gabriel, Serge. Would you like to come to the table?"

"Mmm. It smells good." Serge was hungry and ready to eat. He was always hungry!

Although it is normal for soufflés to sink after a few minutes after coming out of the oven, she wanted to serve them immediately.

The soufflés were ready. As she lifted them out of the oven she was pleased to see that the tops were lightly crisped. She imagined the creamy melting cheese oozing when she dipped her spoon into it. Coating the inside of the ramekin with parmesan cheese before she had poured the mixture in, would make it taste even more cheesy. She quickly decorated the soufflés with a sprinkling of finely-chopped chives and, after placing them on individual serving plates, she directly took them to the table before they sunk. She wanted them to look irresistible as well as tasting delicious. They were just perfect!

Gabriel tasted a spoonful. A burst of the salty Gruyere cheese oozed from the crispy batter and melted on his tongue. He dipped his spoon in again for more soufflé. "Mmm. This is so heavenly, Suzette. The texture is light; not too airy. My taste buds are well and truly tickled. I could eat it forever."

"Thank you. I'm so glad you like it."

"It's delectable", gushed Serge.

"I guess you both approve then?"

She cleared the table and went back into the kitchen, leaving them to talk. Taking the bottle of Limoux out of the fridge, she poured the fizzing, sparkling wine into her crystal glass. Tipping the glass slightly, she took a sip and the bubbles tickled her nose.

It was good to hear Serge laughing. The men were talking about the antics they'd got up to with their friends when they were younger. Suzette could just imagine them - five alluring, young men chatting and flirting with the pretty girls; the *mademoiselles* wouldn't be able to resist their charms. They were all still handsome now, though older and, perhaps, much wiser!

She lifted the salmon parcels and roasted vegetables from out of the oven and left them to rest on the work surface.

She placed the salmon on one end of a white oblong plate, drizzling the lime and ginger marinade over the top. The combination of the lime and the ginger smelled divine. Not wanting to overcook the salmon, she had only baked it for twenty minutes. Next, she took a pair of kitchen tongs and then she carefully arranged the roasted vegetables in a straight line. The red onion, carrot strips, garlic bulbs, green beans and rosemary had crisped on the edges and the colours enhanced the pinkness of the salmon.

Suzette believed that the making of food should not be hurried; it should be made with loving hands. She had an incredible knack of turning fresh vegetables into delicacies that were beyond delicious and would delight anyone's palate. As an artist, she also believed that food should be presented like a piece of artwork, with different textures and flavours to tempt and satisfy the eater. She didn't like the way food was just thrown onto a plate.

Once satisfied with the presentation, she balanced a plate in each hand and served Gabriel and Serge. She collected her own plate and joined them at the table.

Gabriel gazed down at his plate. "What gastronomic delight do we have here, Suzette? It looks so appetising"

"Taste it and give me your opinion", she answered.

As he cut into the salmon it fell into flakes and, when he placed it in his mouth, the tangy zest of the lime intermingled with the spicy ginger, excited him as it caressed his tongue and dissolved. The lightly-scorched edges of the structurally-arranged, balsamic-infused vegetables introduced a sense of flow to the artistic masterpiece and he was tempted further. Deliberately savouring every luscious mouthful, he continued tasting until his plate was empty.

Serge and Suzette had finished eating and they were waiting for his verdict.

"It's a long time since I have tasted anything like what I've just eaten. The flavours, the colours, the visual elements of the food were just perfect."

"I'm so glad you enjoyed it. I relished it too. Suzette has a flair with food and is sensitive with its presentation", Serge commented as he glanced in her direction.

"Merci beaucoup, Suzette. You certainly do have a talent for creating excellent food."

She smiled and nodded, accepting their compliments. Removing the plates from the table, she took them into the kitchen and stacked them; ready for washing later. Noticing that the wine glasses were empty, she uncorked another bottle of chilled Limoux and took it to the table.

"Serge, will you serve our guest some more

wine, whilst I prepare the dessert?"

As a committed Francophile, aware that the French custom is to eat the cheese platter before the dessert, Suzette decided to break with tradition by serving the dessert first – in true British style. They could enjoy the cheeses later.

She removed the syllabub from the fridge and, after placing three shavings of dark chocolate on top, she trickled some ginger liqueur onto the smooth, sublime desserts.

After eating dessert and, not wanting to dominate the conversation with Serge's problems, Suzette made a point of focusing on Gabriel. They talked about his work and his personal life. Suzette consoled him when he discussed his recent break-up with his long-term partner. She was younger than him and she'd wanted to start a family with him. Gabriel already had a daughter and a baby granddaughter. They lived near his ex-wife, who had taken herself off to England to start a new life. He didn't see much of them, although they did speak on the telephone.

"I didn't want any more children. I had to be honest with her. I want to retire next year. It's time for me to explore new avenues."

Serge reflected on the miscarriages that Francesca had endured and he felt quite sad. They had desperately wanted children and he wished he could have had a son of his own. He would have taught him the skills that his own father had taught him. He would have loved him and he would have given him some direction in life. However, he was more than grateful for the relationships he had cultivated with Suzette's two children and her grandchildren. They respected him and they also treated him as if he'd always been part of their family.

Snapping out of his melancholic daydream, he joined in the conversation.

"Do you miss her Gabriel? Do you miss a woman's company, on an intellectual level as well as a physical level?"

Gabriel raised his eyebrows and laughed loudly.

"Trust you to ask me that! Of course, I do. I love female company, especially a woman who has her own opinions and can converse on a variety of topics. Yes, I do miss the physical side, but I am learning more about what I want to do with the rest of my life. I am experiencing a kind of freedom that I have never experienced before and I like it. I want to travel and see other parts of the world."

Both Serge and Suzette nodded and smiled at each other as he continued to explain further about what had recently been happening in his life. She brought the cheese board to the table. Soft ripened Camembert, Gruyere de Comte and Roquefort nestled comfortably alongside grapes, almonds, apricots, figs and chunks of olive bread and slices of baguette.

"An enthusiastic medical graduate has been working with me during the past six months and I have encouraged him to take over my practice. He already knows my patients and is familiar with the locality. If it transpires, then I will make some decisions."

"Well, you've devoted most of your life to caring for others and it's time now to care for yourself."

Listening to Gabriel, Suzette recognised the transformation taking place within Gabriel and was happy for him.

"I do still want to care for others and, I would like to do some voluntary work in the future, but I also know that something is happening to me, urging me to move forward in an entirely different direction."

Reaching for some Roquefort, he spread it thickly onto a chunk of bread and popped it into his mouth.

"I'd would really like to know more about your courses and your therapies. Would it be possible for me to attend one of them?"

"I'm not delivering any group sessions at the moment, but my friend, Eve, is coming over from England in a week's time to complete an intensive programme. I could ask her if you can sit in on a few sessions."

"That would be great. I'm really interested in what you do. Maybe I could bring the medical graduate along with me also?"

Suzette hesitated before answering. "The sessions are personal and very powerful. Maybe you could participate in the programme. It would give you some first-hand experience of the benefits which can be gained from being involved."

Serge smiled as an idea came into his head. Maybe the three of them – himself, Eve and Gabriel could participate in the group sessions.

"If you were able to start the sessions after morning surgery has finished, then maybe I could possibly make it."

Before Suzette could answer, Serge offered his suggestion.

"Why don't you ask your graduate partner to take your surgery? You can be on-call if there are any emergencies. I want to complete the self-actualisation process; so that would make three of us in the group, if you agree."

Suzette glanced over at Serge. Surprised at his suggestion, she didn't question his motive.

"I would need to clear it with Eve first. She is expecting one-to-one sessions.

"What a great idea. I'll speak with him and ask him if he feels confident to take charge of the surgery on his own. I suppose it would be good experience for him."

On reflection, Suzette also thought it would be a useful idea. It could be quite draining when facilitating one-to-one sessions. The transfer of energy within group sessions was far more easier to manage.

"I'll email Eve tomorrow and ask her if she is agreeable to group therapy."

Serge reached for the wine bottle. "More wine?"

Gabriel glanced at his watch. It was eleven fifty-five. The taxi was coming at twelve. Where had the time gone?

"Not for me, thank you. I've had a very pleasant evening. The food was exquisite, the conversation stimulating and my spirit has been uplifted. I've already booked a taxi to collect me at midnight."

No sooner had he spoken, the taxi could be heard pulling up outside. After waving goodbye, they went back into the house. Serge started to clear the table.

"Leave those dishes until the morning, darling. We've had a long day. Let's go to bed."

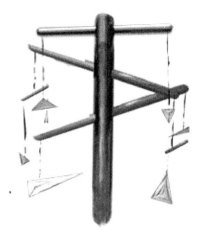

CHAPTER EIGHT

During breakfast they discussed last evening's meal and Gabriel's interest in attending the programme.

"He seemed really interested in it and I don't mind working through the clearing process with him, Suzette."

"I'd better email Eve now, before I forget."

His mind returned to Francesca's illness as he cleared the table. She'd come to him last night in his dreams, telling him once again to let go of his guilt and move on. The intolerable self-reproach over his wife's illness and her passing still weighed heavy and haunted him. He felt that he had put his work before his late wife's illness; even though she had given him his blessing to finish his sculpture. She knew he had to focus on something to help him cope with the unbearable mental torture that was eating away at him. She too was tortured both physically and mentally. It had taken all of her strength to remain strong, but she didn't want her precious husband to endure more torment than he had to.

As he placed the plates into the dishwasher, Francesca spoke to him again. She communicated so clearly that he felt her presence next to him and he could smell her familiar perfume.

"I won't be visiting you as often as I have done. There are things I need to do on the ethereal plane. You have Suzette now and I can see that you have the intention to let go of the negative energy which you've nurtured for the past few years."

He poured the boiling water onto the fresh peppermint leaves in the glass teapot and replaced the lid.

"My decision has been made, Francesca. I'm determined to conquer the pangs of conscience which have penetrated my soul."

"Do it, Serge. I'll watch over you from afar, although you have nothing whatsoever to reproach yourself for."

A draught of cool air brushed past him and she was gone.

Suzette opened her laptop and clicked into

her email account. Several emails were unopened but she would do it later. Opening Eve's last email she began to type, explaining that she would collect her from the airport and asking her if she would mind if two others joined her on the course – Serge and Serge's friend.

Ending the email with *'Let me know what you think. Look forward to seeing you soon. Suzette xxx',* she closed her laptop and returned to the kitchen.

The smell of the peppermint infusion didn't mask the odour of the familiar fragrance that sometimes permeated the confines of their home. She knew that Francesca had visited again.

Pouring the infusion into two mugs, she sensed his unease and allowed him to collect his thoughts before making conversation.

"I've never shown you a photograph of Francesca, have I? Would you like to see her?"

He was correct. He'd never shown her a photograph of his late wife, but she knew exactly what she looked like.

He opened a large tin box. Suzette waited patiently whilst he sifted through a plethora of photographs.

"No. I did notice when I first came into your house that you hadn't displayed any photographs of her. However, I did deduce that the figurative sculpture outside was an image of Francesca."

"It was far too upsetting for me to have photographs of her around. I've always kept a small photograph of her in my wallet, although it is a bit tatty now."

He'd never spoken in depth to Suzette about his late wife and Suzette had never pursued it; sensing how distressing it was for him.

"Here she is. This is when I first met her. She was twenty two at the time. This one was in her early thirties, just after she had endured yet another miscarriage. You can see the traces of sadness in her eyes. We wanted children so much. She would have been an excellent mother. It never did happen the way we wanted it to."

A tiny white butterfly hovered around them and landed on the table near to where they were sitting. It stayed there, as if it was listening to the conversation.

Taking the photographs out of his hand, she studied them closely. In one of the photographs, Francesca looked exactly like the spirit who had come to visit her on several occasions. Her dark hairstyle, her hypnotising almond-shaped eyes and her sensual figure was not dissimilar to Sophia Loren's appearance.

He placed another photograph in her hand.

"This is just before she was diagnosed with lung cancer. We'd just returned from a holiday on the Amalfi Coast. She looked happy there, don't you think?"

Suzette could see a deep sense of sadness in Francesca's eyes. The camera had captured her aura and several orbs were clearly visible in the background; a sign of spiritual energy. She wondered whether Francesca had known then about the cancer and had chosen not to say anything to Serge.

"She did look happy, Serge. She was a very beautiful woman", she added.

The familiar fragrance wafted around them and the tiny butterfly took flight.

"She was, Suzette. Not only on the outside was she beautiful; she was beautiful on the inside too. She was so very caring and non-judgemental towards others. She always looked for the good in a person. Her relentless, charitable work went unnoticed and that was how she wanted it."

Emotionally congested, tears welled in his eyes and he allowed his vulnerability to surface. He sobbed.

She acknowledged his outpouring. It was part of the healing process. He was of the era where men didn't cry. Hegemonic tradition forbade it. If a man shed tears, he would somehow be deemed to be less of a man. Yet, she'd often seen the emotional side of her husband. He'd cried tears of happiness at their wedding last year.

"The lung cancer had been a slow-growing one. She'd been coughing all the time – in fact, it seemed like she'd always had a chesty cough. She thought it may be due to her allergies. She had never smoked a cigarette in her life. Neither of us smoked."

Serge drained the last dregs of peppermint

infusion from his mug, before continuing.

"She'd tried endless organic remedies and complementary medicines. She'd also had several courses of chemotherapy treatment, but she couldn't tolerate the sickness and the feelings of weakness that came with it; and the loss of her hair was also extremely difficult for her to accept. It was a terrible time for her."

Suzette's father had also been diagnosed with a slow-growing lung cancer, so she knew a little about the cruel condition. She refrained from talking about him; not because it was emotional for her (and it was), but because her husband had finally 'opened up' and, it was his time to disclose.

"When the oncologist informed her that the cancer had spread and that secondaries had been revealed on the x-rays, she knew then that she didn't want any more treatment. She wanted to be at home with me. I looked after her, with the help of a nurse who visited regularly to check her progress. She died in my arms. I was so grateful that the cancer had not reached her brain. I have to admit that when she died, a part of me died also."

She passed the photographs back to him and he placed them in the tin. Looking across at Suzette, he wondered how she felt about what he had just revealed. He had no intention of hurting her. She had been and still was, more than accepting of his melancholic moods and he was appreciative of her considerate approach to his lengthy periods of silence.

"Why don't you frame some of these photographs? You know, you shouldn't hide them away."

He thought for a moment. "You don't mind me doing that?"

"Why would I mind, darling? She's been with you for a large part of your life and she still is, in spirit. We'll look for some suitable frames when we go into Narbonne."

He stood up and walked towards where she was sitting.

"Hold me, ma chèrie. Hold me tight and don't let me go back to where I've been for the last few years."

His hand brushed the unruly curls that were falling onto her face and he tenderly placed a kiss on her lips.

She did as he bade her. She held him close. Her husband had made his decision to heal himself.

"Come on, let's walk the labyrinth before we have lunch. We both have much work to do this afternoon."

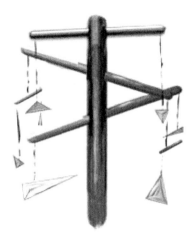

CHAPTER NINE

The kitchen terrace provided welcome shade from the searing heat of the midday sun. They had just finished eating their lunch when the muffled sound of familiar voices grew louder as Hugo and his mother, Nicole, approached the entrance to the courtyard.

Serge rushed to assist Hugo, who was struggling to navigate his mother's cumbersome wheelchair across the bumpy, gravel driveway. Her mobility was limited now.

Ten years earlier, Nicole Rocher had been diagnosed with early-onset Parkinson's Disease at the age of forty-eight. Hugo was only nine years old.

At the time of diagnosis, Nicole's husband decided that he couldn't possibly cope with her degenerative disorder, as well as managing the challenges of Hugo's autism. He'd left them to survive on their own and had taken himself off to America to start a new life. He did, however, provide for them with a huge, yearly monetary allowance, so that they could engage the necessary support and also live a fairly comfortable lifestyle.

Pre-diagnosis, Nicole had been experiencing intermittent low moods and several panic attacks. Her movements were a bit shaky and she was slower to react, both on a physical level and mental level. Initially, she had thought that the symptoms were those of approaching menopause and had been devastated when the specialist doctor in Narbonne had sensitively informed her that she had an incurable disease.

Hugo, not surprisingly, didn't cope well with the change when his father deserted them; nor could he handle the changes in his mother's health. At first, he hadn't much empathy for the pain his mother endured, but she knew only too well, that it was part of who Hugo was – it was part of his autism.

He reacted angrily to his father's departure and would aggressively challenge anyone who mentioned his father's name; let alone ask about the circumstances which led to him leaving.

To deal with the unwanted changes, he developed his own routine of daily responsibilities; namely ensuring that his mother had the necessary things to hand, so that it didn't cause her too much stress when he wasn't with her. He was an expert at solving problems.

Subconsciously, his concern for his mother, in relation to his previous behaviour of lacking empathy, was manifesting itself in a way that was most unusual for him. He had begun to express his feelings and thoughts about developments and challenges in his life; another aspect which he hadn't previously vocalised or focused on.

Hugo had taken on the responsibility of being a young carer to his mother. One reason was that he didn't like the intrusion of others in his personal domain. Another reason was that he had developed an extreme closeness with his mother, knowing that her condition was incurable and he wanted to make every moment count – for her and for him.

His behaviour astounded Nicole, who had watched her precious, only son grow up with many sensory and social challenges. As a child, he hadn't spoken a coherent word until he was three years old. He hadn't particularly liked being cuddled and was emotionally distant from her and others around him. Now, here he was, caring for her in an adult way and he was verbally proclaiming his love for her, several times a day. The change in his personality was extraordinary and she revelled in his loving attentiveness and his progress. It was something that she thought she would never, ever experience. It was as if her illness had forced the change.

His lack of attendance at school alerted the child protection department, who thought he was at risk because of his circumstances at home. They also considered that his education was being compromised, even though Hugo was a high-functioning, autistic young man with an IQ score of 118 and an enhanced learning ability in subjects which were of interest to him.

They even wanted to take him into care, fearing that he was socially under-developed. They didn't fully understand the symptoms of autism; neither did they choose to understand!

With the help of two legal advisers, Nicole challenged their dogmatic principles and, after the judicial system had addressed the situation, it was decided that it would be detrimental to the mental well-being of Hugo and Nicole if they were to be separated.

As he was achieving highly on an academic level, it was also decided that he should attend school five half-days per week and complete work at home. His progress would be monitored by the school social worker, who would also monitor his social development.

Hugo had been labelled at school by bullies who thought he was an oddity. Some of his teachers were also of the same opinion; although there was one teacher who understood him. That teacher had been instrumental in permitting Hugo to attend school on a part-time basis.

They'd first met their next-door neighbours ten months previously. Nicole had heard that Suzette had some past experience of special educational needs and approached her to discreetly discuss her son's level of ability. She wanted to ensure that he was given every opportunity to further achieve, both academically and socially, before she passed away. Her illness was progressing swiftly and she had a feeling that her neighbours would take him 'under their wings'. She was right.

Serge had instantly been concerned for Hugo's welfare. Seeing the haunting look of sadness in the young man's eyes, reminded him of his own sorrow. He knew also that he'd been given a chance to show love and understanding. Over time, the two of them had gradually developed a deep, meaningful connection through their own experiences and loss.

Serge's own sorrowful experiences allowed him to empathise with the impending deterioration of his situation regarding his mother's health. Getting to know Hugo had given him an unexpected opportunity to fill the gap of not having a son; a son that he had desperately yearned for. The role of father-figure had slowly evolved since their first meeting. They'd both spent many afternoons discussing and debating various current issues and theorists. His life had more significance to it, because of his influence on Hugo's life.

However, from Hugo's perspective, the newly-found friendship was difficult. His inability to make new friends and his social awkwardness had proved to be challenging. Not only did he not recognise when Serge was joking with him, he also interpreted his words literally. He couldn't read his facial expressions or his body language. It was hard for Hugo to read social cues.

In spite of the differences, the unspoken father and son relationship had developed and, when Hugo wouldn't make eye contact during discussions, Serge learnt that it wasn't because he was disinterested; it was because of his autistic difficulties with communication and social skills. Careful choice of words were used, in case they were wrongly misinterpreted. After a tentative start, both soon became comfortable with each other's company.

Suzette had also welcomed the opportunity to be 'of service' to her neighbours. In England she'd had frequent contact with many individuals who had learning differences and disabilities. It had been a mission of hers to make people aware of the value of respecting differences and she promoted the benefits of an inclusive society. It was still, very much, her mission!

Hugo embraced his neighbours.

"Bonjour."

"Bonjour Hugo", they both answered in unison.

Serge bent down and embraced Nicole.
"Bonjour Nicole."

She welcomed his embrace, nodding in acknowledgement.

"Grateful for another day", she mumbled.

Suzette also leant over her. "You look wonderful today, Nicole. It's so lovely to see you. Come, let's have a drink."

They made their way over to the kitchen terrace. Serge took a bottle of chilled Limoux from the fridge and popped the cork. Together they toasted each other and, whilst the men engaged in a healthy discussion about the effects of the global economy and environmental issues, Nicole and Suzette moved to an area of the garden where they could speak in private.

A contemplative awareness was palpable before Nicole spoke in her incomprehensible tone.

"Suzette, can I ask you something?"

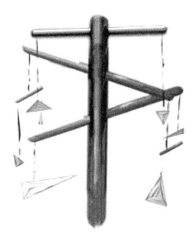

CHAPTER TEN

After Hugo and Nicole had left, Serge went to his studio to work on his sculpture. It had to be completed in three days. The transporter and crane would arrive on Thursday to take it to its destination in Northern France.

Suzette opened her laptop and checked her emails. Four new emails were in the inbox. One was from her daughter, updating her on the news from England and asking her when she would be free to FaceTime. Another email was from Eve, agreeing to participate in the group sessions and confirming the flight arrival time in Carcassonne. The other two were junk mail.

After replying to her daughter and Eve, she clicked onto the document entitled 'Novel Number Four'. She really did have to exercise her writing muscles and finish her latest book. She'd only three more chapters to complete and proof-read before mailing it to her publisher for a further proof-reading and editing.

The document quickly opened and she manoeuvred the mouse onto the last page that she'd previously been working on. Scribbles on post-it notes and several hand-written pages of text were stacked in neat piles on her writing desk, alongside the already printed copies of her nearly-finished novel.

She picked up her notes to commence typing up Chapter Thirty-Two and put them down again. Her thoughts were filled with what Nicole had told her earlier on. Even though she knew that her condition had deteriorated quickly over the last few months, she hadn't wanted to think about the inevitable. She'd developed a close friendship with mother and son and an emotional attachment had developed.

Although initially depressed at the onset of her illness, Nicole had managed to remain positive, with the benefit of daily doses of anti-depressants. The same positive attitude was now wearing very thin. The cocktail of medicines that she took were having little effect on her mental and physical wellbeing. Her quality of life was declining rapidly. Doctors were concerned with the way her illness was presenting itself and had advised her that she was in the final stages.

She knew that her body was breaking down; as was her mind. She had experienced hallucinations and dreamt that she was floating up to heaven with her guardian angel at her side. Her confused state of mind and her loss of memory was a constant worry for Hugo, who was finding it difficult to manage her symptoms.

The incontinence and frequency of urinary tract infections were an embarrassment for her. Not wanting to cause Hugo more distress than was necessary, she would sit uncomfortably in her own mess until her nurse arrived to change her clothes and wash her.

Initially, communicating with Nicole was somewhat difficult for Suzette, due to her speech problems and severe body spasms.

Later, however, she knew exactly what to do and say to offer support.

Even though Suzette had told her that she looked well when she'd seen her earlier, she was alarmed by Nicole's drastic weight loss and the pallor of her skin.

On her usual morning visit, the nurse had advised that it would be best if Nicole had a feeding tube fitted to prevent her from choking, as her swallowing had become difficult.

Suzette's mind was in a whirl as she recalled

her friend's fractured words "Suzette, can I ask you something?" She knew what she was going to tell her and what she going to ask; and the answer was a definite YES.

Nicole had asked if they would support Hugo emotionally and look out for his welfare after she had passed over. She knew that his autism and his need to be alone would manifest itself and she didn't want him to be lonely. She also knew that her son had felt a sense of belonging with Serge and Suzette. They'd made him feel as if he mattered. They'd listened to him and he respected and valued their friendship.

Tears dripped down Suzette's cheeks as she thought of how brave Nicole had been; bringing up her son on her own whilst enduring a debilitating illness.

She clicked onto the 'close' icon and exited her work. She couldn't concentrate. Making her way to the studio, she saw Serge walking towards her. His troubled look said it all. He also knew.

He took her hand in his and they crossed the stream in silence. On reaching the clearing, they sat down inside the summer house, side by side, regaling their own versions of their neighbour's visit. In spite of Hugo's initial reluctance to talk about his feelings, he'd openly divulged his fears to Serge. He knew that his mother was dying and he also knew that it would be imminent. Serge had hugged him and reassured him of his and Suzette's support and he'd cried.

"I just knew what she was going to tell me", Suzette disclosed.

"Her time has come. She's ready to go. Her body's very weak and so is her mind. She's been hanging on to her life for Hugo's sake. She knows that we'll look after him."

Taking hold of his hand, she led Serge to the opening of the labyrinth. Both silently stated their intentions and started to tread the marble path.

The smaller oscillating triangles which hung from the larger mobiles quivered, as if reminding them of the impending changes.

Suzette offered up her thoughts.

"Please Lord, help Nicole to have a peaceful and pain-free passing."

"Please help Hugo to cope with the trauma of losing his maman." Serge prayed fervently.

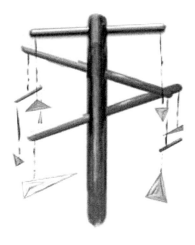

CHAPTER ELEVEN

The previous day's encounter weighed heavily on Suzette and Serge's emotions. The approaching sadness, which would have an irrevocable effect on Hugo's life, was difficult to take in. They wondered how he'd react. In previous times of stress he'd been known to display anger and aggression. What they did know was that they would support him and love him. He would come to live with them for as long as he liked. Suzette had made a promise to Nicole and she would honour that promise.

Deadlines were seriously looming for both of them and focusing on finalising their work would be difficult.

After their daily visit to the labyrinth, they went their separate ways; Serge to his studio and Suzette to her writing room.

Having other things on his mind, Serge had procrastinated over the past few weeks. In truth, he knew that he had been delaying work on his sculpture, so that he would gratefully experience that tantalising thrill of the adrenaline rush that working under pressure brings. It was a feeling which he relished and cherished.

He reflected on how he'd transformed the block of marble into a magnificent piece of art. In his eyes, all of his pieces were magnificent. They were a part of him and he loved every sculpture that he'd created; remaining confidently oblivious to negative criticism of his abstracted forms.

Within his secluded zone, inside his studio, nothing else mattered except the completion of his work. He switched on the ventilation system to filter the dust, which would be instantly airborne once he'd started the smoothing process.

After putting on his fully-encased face mask and special ultra-thin gloves, he stroked the base of the sculpture, feeling for any unwanted ridges and imperfections. His work had been completed on the top half of the sculpture several weeks ago. The scaffolding had been removed once he was satisfied with the smooth finish.

The sculpture spoke to him as he carefully explored, caressed and smoothed each area.

"Touch me. Come closer, I need you", the sculpture beckoned.

Serge performed his tactile acts of love and the marble surrendered to his delicate, lover's touch. Amorously, he imagined the sculpture sighing in appreciation of his strokes. A seductive smile involuntarily spread across his face as he gently moved the sandpaper and cloth in unhurried backward and forward movements, intentionally lingering on specific areas to ensure a smooth finish was achieved. The process was fulfilling for Serge, especially when the polished sheen on the marble revealed intricate patterns on its surface.

Standing back for a moment, he lifted the visor on his mask and swigged from the bottle of water he'd left on the floor nearby. The ventilation system whirred in the background, serenading him and urging him to continue with his romantic act of love.

He whispered seductively to his creation as he replaced the worn-out gloves with a new pair and pulled down his visor.

"I'm not ignoring you; I'm just replenishing my energy."

Serge wanted to prolong the smoothing process; arduously clinging onto the mounting passion that would increase with each touch, until the gratifying climax occurred when the sculpture was finished. The intense, intimate relationship between sculptor and sculpture would then cease and a tinge of sadness would taint the sense of achievement.

But, for the moment, he delighted in the fact that it would take at least another full day to complete his work. He would savour every sensual moment until the end. In peaceful contemplation, he allowed his mind to wander. He felt both privileged and grateful to be doing something that he loved. His talent had enabled him to fulfil his ambitions and also touch the lives of others with his artistic perspective.

Meanwhile, within the secluded confines of her writing room, Suzette's deft fingers frantically touch-typed their way through the last chapters. She'd eagerly let her imagination run wild as she played with the vocabulary; deleting sentences and editing paragraphs until she was satisfied. She knew that once she had proof-read her final draft, there would be several more amendments to be made.

Writer's block had been a frequent visitor to her recently. On many occasions she would sit down to write, but the words she had previously stored inside her head would not materialise into anything worth reading.

There'd been moments of intense creativity when she'd been woken in the early hours of the morning, with ideas dancing around her head. It was, at those productive times, that she would scribble furiously, embracing the words which flowed freely and easily. Those distinct moments of inspiration could last for several days and, although her eyes would sting with lack of sleep and her body ached, she would continue writing until her belly groaned with hunger, whilst the need to slake her thirst would leave her weak and nauseous.

Such was her juxtaposed obsession. It was an 'all or nothing' fixation that fed her and starved her at the same time. Everyone and everything would be neglected when her addiction captured her and held her in its grasp.

She pressed 'save' and clicked on 'print'. The printer churned out the final chapters and Suzette stapled them, before placing them with the previously printed chapters.

A sigh of relief whistled through her pursed lips. She switched off her laptop and made her way to the kitchen. The proof-reading could wait until tomorrow. She needed to eat!

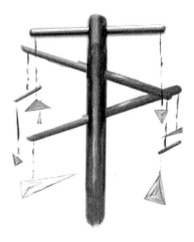

CHAPTER TWELVE

The Couture household had been a hive of activity. Serge had completed his sculpture. Suzette had proof-read the closing chapters of her novel and emailed it to the publisher. The house had been prepared for Eve's visit and the self-actualisation course. Resources had been printed off for each session and menus had been prepared and baking done for the days ahead.

No matter how busy they had been, they still made time to visit Nicole and Hugo, once in the morning and again in the evening. They were concerned for their neighbours' welfare.

Hugo opened the door and invited them in. Although he appeared to be coping, Suzette noticed how gaunt he looked; more so today than previous days. His once broad and muscular frame was now lean and his posture was stooped. He'd been losing weight since his mother had confessed the severity of her illness and his clothes hung loosely from his body. He'd allowed his dark, curly hair to grow long and he looked unkempt.

He returned to his mother's side and sat next to her on the bed. He'd hardly left her side and had even brought her bed downstairs so that she could see her garden through the full-length windows. He knew it would bring her pleasure. Previously, when she had been healthier, she'd liked nothing better than pottering around her garden, tending to the flowers and the plants.

"Bonjour Nicole."

Nicole moved her head slightly.

Hugo stood up. Taking a hairbrush from the bedside table, he gently brushed his mother's hair. With skilled expertise, he gathered her hair into a chignon to stop it from falling over her face. Then he took some lavender body lotion and tenderly massaged it into her arms and her hands. She murmured something and smiled at her precious son, in appreciation of his attention.

Suzette observed how this young man seemed to have grown up overnight. It was painful to watch him tenderly caring for his mother. His endearing gestures touched her.

"Has the nurse been?" Serge asked.

"Yes, she left just before you arrived. She'll return at four, or earlier if she is needed."

The nurse looked after Nicole's personal needs, but he insisted on caring for his mother in every other way. She was all he had. His father still transferred a monthly allowance into the joint account which he and his mother shared, but he never telephoned them or wrote to enquire about Nicole's state of health. Hugo didn't even know where he lived. He'd even forgotten what he looked like.

When Nicole realised the extent of her incapacity, she'd transferred the house into Hugo's name and had written a will leaving all she owned to her only son.

Hugo wrote some poetry and recited it to his mother. He also concocted several stories to brighten her day; always observing her closely for any signs of deterioration.

"Are you comfortable, Maman?"

Her tired eyes glistened with pride as she looked at him and nodded. Her speech was non-existent now, except for a quiet murmur which was indecipherable; although Hugo seemed to know exactly what his mother said and needed. Yes, she was comfortable knowing that he was taking care of her. She wasn't frightened to die. She knew now that it was her time to leave this earth. Suzette and Serge had promised that they would support Hugo and she knew that they wouldn't break their promise.

Serge emptied the contents of the large, cardboard box onto the kitchen table. Suzette had prepared his meals for the day and made some *aux amandes* biscuits to try and tempt him to eat.

Hugo didn't leave the house now, except to pick flowers from the garden for his mother. He was scared that she would die alone if he left her. He even slept on the sofa, so he could be near her; listening for her every sound.

"These meals have been freshly cooked this morning. You must try to eat something, Hugo. You will need to keep up your strength to look after your maman."

"Thank you. I'll try, but I don't have that much of an appetite.

Nicole uttered something and nodded her head slightly.

"I will, Maman." He'd try to eat something, if only for her peace of mind.

Suzette sat down on the armchair beside Nicole's bed, chatting idly about things that had been happening. Nicole's complexion was pallid and the hollows of her cheeks were wrinkled with the extremity of her weight loss. She was now being drip-fed through a tube in her nose and her medication was administered into her body by means of a cannula in her arm. The last time she had tried to eat a little food, she nearly choked. Hugo had been terrified and rang the doctor who came immediately and wanted to transfer Nicole to hospital. She refused to go. She'd previously told Hugo that when it was her time to go, she wanted to die at home. She wanted to spend the rest of her days with her son, in private.

Having communicated his mother's wish, the doctor reluctantly agreed to a nurse attending more regularly to monitor her. Hugo should call him at any time if he was concerned. The doctor had recently lost his own mother and he could empathise with how Hugo was feeling.

Whilst Suzette was with Nicole, Serge and Hugo went into the garden, to discuss concerns.

"Ring me anytime you need to; day or night. I'll always have my mobile with me. Don't feel that you are alone. Remember that we're here for you. You've become part of our family. We love you. I love you. You're like the son I never had."

Serge held him close. It didn't make Hugo feel any better. He felt empty and wanted to die with his mother.

On returning inside the house, they found Suzette browsing through the anthology of poems and Nicole was sleeping.

"I think we should leave now, Suzette. The carriers are due to arrive at midday."

After saying farewell, they walked in silence back to their home. No words were needed. The tears that blurred their vision, said all that needed to be said.

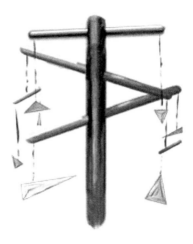

CHAPTER THIRTEEN

The combined transporter and crane arrived fifteen minutes early. The driver had somehow managed to miss the traffic tailbacks that had been building up on the motorways.

Preparation for the lengthy journey had commenced six months ago. Risk assessments had been undertaken and special permission had been obtained to allow the wide transporter to travel on the motorways. A detailed gantt chart showing the sequence of events, together with photographs and instructions for packing, had been prepared.

Luckily, the driveway had a strong concrete

sub-base under the gravel to take the weight of the vehicles. Serge had previously used this specialist carrier and he was confident with the service they provided, which included the necessary insurance and a fleet of escort vehicles.

With exact precision, the heavy sculpture was safely lifted onto the transporter and placed onto a protective base. An enormous crate was constructed around it and then it was filled with packing materials, before being securely closed.

Serge's feelings were mixed; sad that he would no longer be working with it and elated with his finished piece of art. Although he was slightly anxious about the journey, he was relieved that the sculpture had been securely packed away, without any damage.

The carrier had promised to telephone him, to confirm delivery when they'd reached their destination. The sculpture would be taken to a secure storage area before being installed in the atrium of the company's headquarters. The official unveiling would be in ten days. Serge and Suzette would be the guests of honour at the ceremony; although neither of them courted the limelight. They preferred to remain in the background.

After Suzette had given the drivers a variety of sandwiches and bottles of water for their return journey, they both walked back into the house.

Serge sighed heavily. Exhausted, he sat down on one of the comfy chairs on the kitchen terrace.

"I think we both deserve some champagne, Serge. Don't you?"

She took the chilled, pink Moutard from the fridge, placed it in an ice bucket and went outside. Slightly tilting the bottle, she rotated it before gently releasing the cork. As she poured the fizzing, liquid decadence into the crystal glasses, the millions of tiny, aromatic molecules whooshed before cascading their way back up to the top. Raising their glasses, they congratulated each other on their achievements.

"To us, Serge."

"To our success and happiness, my darling."

The tinkling of crystal was a frequent sound in their house. The glasses were the ones they'd drank champagne from on their wedding day. They'd belonged to Serge's parents who'd also drank champagne from them on their own wedding day. They held very special memories.

As the cold champagne entered her mouth, Suzette savoured the effervescent bubbles as they dissipated on her tongue, before swallowing the delicate, pink liquid. The intensity of the instantly seductive fruitiness lingered in her mouth.

She submerged the half-empty bottle into the ice-filled bucket and went inside to collect the lunch she'd prepared earlier.

They spoke of their recent accomplishments whilst hungrily indulging themselves on a late lunch of fresh figs with herbed goat's cheese, stuffed olives with walnuts and garlic, cheese and onion tartlets and strawberries sprinkled with black pepper.

Serge topped up the glasses and placed the empty bottle back inside the ice bucket, whilst Suzette cleared the table.

Returning to the terrace, she gently touched his shoulder before taking another sip of champagne. Even though she'd eaten plenty, she felt somewhat tipsy as the euphoric sensation stimulated her intensified hormones.

Serge leant over and kissed her lingeringly. She shivered. The tender touch of his lips always excited her. Instinctively, she knew exactly what was about to happen. He took hold of her left hand and sensually stroked the inside of her wrist, whilst holding her gaze. She could feel her pulse quickening.

"Drink your champagne, Suzette. We have an appointment with pleasure."

Emptying their glasses, they went indoors. Like newlyweds, they excitedly rushed upstairs, anticipating and imagining the joining together of their sexually charged bodies.

The Cancerian woman and the Leo man were compatible on both a physical and emotional level; always making an effort to please each other and showing each other the depth of their love. Their anticipation did not disappoint, as they spent the afternoon satisfying each other's needs.

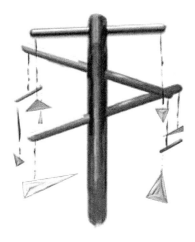

CHAPTER FOURTEEN

Eve Elliot's flight was on time. She'd expected a bumpy landing and it was one. The runway at Carcassonne airport is short and the pilots always had to brake quickly. For first time visitors to the airport, their landing experience was frightening. Children and adults alike screamed loudly as the plane came to an abrupt halt.

Eve wondered why the cabin crew didn't prewarn the passengers about the runway. Every time she'd travelled to this airport, never once had she heard an announcement of this type.

As she stepped from the aircraft the intense

Mediterranean heat caught her unawares and, momentarily, took her breath away. When she'd left Manchester it had been pouring down with rain and was quite cold.

She was looking forward to seeing Suzette. They'd first met ten years ago when they'd worked on an educational project. It had been a great success and they'd remained close friends.

Although curious, Eve was still apprehensive about completing the self-actualisation process. She understood that it was about clearing the past and moving forward with your life. Well, maybe apprehensive was the wrong adjective to use; she was bloody scared!

She ambled through passport control and collected her luggage. The small arrivals area was crowded, but she spotted Suzette immediately. They rushed towards each other and embraced.

"Eve. It's so lovely to see you. It's been ages. I've been so looking forward to you coming. Serge is preparing lunch for us."

"Me too. Once I'd made my decision, I couldn't wait to get here. Hey, you look great. That man of yours must be looking after you well."

She grinned and rolled her eyes. "Oh. He is. He definitely is!"

Eve knew exactly what she was implying. They had the same cheeky sense of humour and were in sync with each other; to the point of answering for each other and also knowing what each other was thinking.

"Come on. I'm parked over the road. It won't take us too long. The roads didn't seem too busy on my way here."

Eve felt nostalgic. She'd holidayed in the Languedoc area several times before and had once thought she might like to buy a small property near Olvano. It had always been a vision of hers, but she'd been too scared to take the chance.

They drove past La Cite de Carcassone. The castle held fond memories for Eve. She'd eaten at a restaurant there with an interesting man she'd had a holiday fling with. She smiled to herself as she remembered the thrilling encounter. It was one which she'd never ever forget. She'd nearly allowed herself to fall in love with him. Nearly! Her common sense prevailed and she took it for what it was – a holiday romance. They'd kept in touch for a while, but it had fizzled out. Long distance relationships were difficult to maintain, unless you were very lucky. Suzette had said that she'd let him 'slip through her fingers', but she'd known that it wouldn't work. She'd had that gut feeling.

"How's everyone back home?" Suzette enquired.

"You know. Same as it always is. I'm sick of same; that's why I'm here now. Anyhow, what's this man like? The one who's on the course with me? Is he handsome?"

"Oh. I'm sure you'll like him, Eve. You'll meet him tomorrow. I've invited him to dinner."

Eve raised her eyebrows and grinned at her. "Come on. What's he like?"

"Wait and see. I'm sure he will be to your taste, Madame."

"You seem really settled here. I've always admired how you took yourself off and did what you wanted to do."

"What's life about if you don't take risks? You exist. You don't live. I'm so lucky living here in France. The lifestyle is what I've always wanted. I love it here."

"The same old philosophical Suzette." Eve chuckled.

"Hey you. Less of the old! A lady in her early sixties isn't old. I'm in my prime. Serge will definitely vouch for that."

Laughter erupted as Suzette took a short cut down a country lane. The vines would soon be ready for picking. Some of the wine growers still picked their grapes by hand and they employed holidaymakers or their friends to help them with harvesting. It was a laborious task but they felt it was less damaging to the grapes. They tended their vines with love and they would harvest their grapes in the same manner.

"I'm sure he would, Madame Couture!"

Serge was relaxing on the bench beside the stream, reading an article on mindfulness. He practised mindfulness daily; sometimes alone and at other times with Suzette. Just looking out from where he was sitting, the panoramic view was so breathtakingly beautiful; a view he never tired of. He'd made the right choice to buy the property when it had come up for sale.

Deep in thought, he pondered on the last few years of his life. He'd experienced many emotions; sorrow, anger, success, trust, love and passion. He'd also experienced deep depression and he still harboured feelings of guilt and regret; triggered by Francesca's cancer and her subsequent death. But then Suzette had appeared and something magical happened. She'd given him his life back.

Perusing the article further, he read – 'Mindfulness does not work for men. Cultural expectations and hegemonic traditions prevent it from working, since the male and female species deal with emotional stress in completely different ways'.

As a male, Serge couldn't know fully how a woman dealt with stress. He knew that Suzette emitted positive energy – lots of it – and she'd take herself off to the clearing to tread the labyrinth if she felt stressed; to ruminate and unravel her thoughts.

'Men will side-step and cause distractions, rather than face up to emotional issues', the article continued.

"That part was right", he spoke aloud. He'd also distracted himself with many things rather than acknowledge his true feelings. It had caused his mental health to suffer. Alcohol had lured him into its den and kept him prisoner for a while. The alcohol had numbed his feelings but it had also sent him crazy. He'd felt extremely vulnerable.

Speaking aloud again, he argued with no one in particular, "I disagree with some of this. Mindfulness does work for men. It's helped me."

As Suzette pulled up on the driveway, he got up from the bench and walked over to greet them.

Kissing Eve on both cheeks, he welcomed her. "Bonjour Eve. It's so nice to meet you again. I hardly had a chance to speak with you at the wedding."

Kissing Suzette firmly on her lips, he joked. "And nice to see you too, ma chérie."

After collecting Eve's luggage, he followed Suzette and Eve onto the terrace.

"Sit down, ladies. Lunch will be served soon. A glass of Limoux, perhaps?"

Suzette nodded.

Eve replied, "That would be very nice. Thank you."

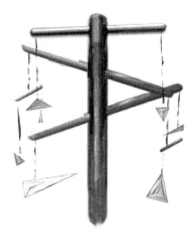

CHAPTER FIFTEEN

Eve had slept soundly. The luxurious king-size bed with its white linen sheets, infused with a calming scent of lavender, might have been the reason. Or could it have been the several glasses of Limoux that she'd imbibed the previous evening! Despite the latter, she felt refreshed and was looking forward to dinner later when she'd meet Gabriel.

The fine aroma of freshly-percolated coffee wafting up the stairs, enticed her out of bed.

Walking towards the window she could see the narrow stream and part of the lush vegetable garden. In the distance, she observed the Pyrenees and the rolling vineyards. A shivering sensation of *déjà vu* washed over her. There was something about the Languedoc culture that she loved. It felt like home. She'd holidayed in Trebes and Olvano several times and the friendly villagers had always welcomed her.

She quickly showered and stepped into some denim shorts and dragged a navy, sleeveless tee shirt over her head. She really needed that coffee, now!

Suzette and Serge were sat outside. A variety of breads, cheeses and confitures adorned the long table, along with the precious coffee percolator.

"Bonjour Madame," Serge greeted her.

"Bonjour Eve. Coffee?" enquired Suzette.

She went over and embraced them both. The sun was just starting to come around onto the terrace and she welcomed the warmth on her skin.

"Good morning. Oh! Yes please."

"Help yourself to breakfast. We've waited for you."

"Thanks. I think I'll need a few cups of coffee first."

Serge and Suzette reached for the bread and cheese and started to eat, whilst Eve poured the steaming, black liquid into her cup.

"Did you sleep well?" Serge asked, after swallowing a chunk of walnut bread.

"I've had the most wonderful sleep. The best I've had in a long time. That bed of yours is so comfortable."

He chuckled, remembering the lengthy conversations they'd had the evening before. Eve had candidly discussed her romantic encounters and much laughter had taken place.

"I bet your head didn't touch the pillow before you were fast asleep. We managed to get through quite a few bottles of wine yesterday."

Eve tried to recollect the previous evening. She remembered clearly that she'd eaten mouth-watering food, drank fine wines in excellent company and discussed matters relating to current issues in the world; but couldn't remember much else!

"This coffee tastes quite nutty. I really like it. Is it French?"

Suzette raised her eyebrows.

"You should like it. I've had it shipped over from England. It's your favourite."

She laughed. "It tastes so much better over here, though."

Reaching for some bread, she spread a large helping of Roquefort thickly onto it.

After two further cups of coffee and lots more bread, cheese and apricot confiture, she leant back in her chair and surveyed the large expanse of garden. She felt so relaxed.

Sitting for a while, they chatted about friends and family back in England. Serge spoke about some of his work and his exhibitions. Eve was fascinated when she heard that some of his sculptures were inspired by Henry Moore. She loved going to Yorkshire Sculpture Park to see his magnificent pieces of work.

Serge interrupted her train of thought.

"Would you like to join us in our special place, Eve?"

Intrigued by his invitation, she raised her eyebrows and nodded her head; wondering what this special place would be like!

Serge cleared the remainder of the food from the table. After locking the door, he took hold of Suzette and Eve's hands and guided them towards the narrow stream, glistening with iridescent pebbles.

As Eve looked into the stream, it reminded her of the many times her and Suzette had gone on their weekend walks in the countryside. Even though Eve was the taller of the two, she always managed to misjudge the width of the stream they had to cross and, almost always, fell in. She glanced at Suzette and nodded; knowing exactly what she was thinking.

Stepping over the stream and, in single file with Serge leading at the front, they ambled along the winding path; stopping at certain points so that Serge could enlighten Eve with the names of the many different fruit and nut trees which inhabited the orchard.

"The lavender I used to make my wedding bouquet was from this exact plant", informed Suzette.

Eve smiled, pleased her to see her friend so happy.

The fragrances confined within the orchard were so soothing and, as the late morning sun cast its rays through the gaps in the trees, Eve felt calm.

As they entered the clearing, Eve couldn't believe what was in front of her. She stood back in amazement. She'd not expected this! To the right of her stood a superb free-standing sculpture. She knew it was Calder-inspired by the colours and the shapes. She was mesmerised by the red, yellow and white triangles of different sizes swaying backwards and forwards.

She looked towards Suzette. "You?" she whispered. She felt she had to whisper in this undisturbed clearing.

Suzette nodded.

To the left, stood a summer house and, almost parallel with the oscillating sculpture, an impressive labyrinth welcomed her; lulling her to come closer. In the centre of the labyrinth, stood a triangular water sculpture; its clear water drizzling down the three sides into a channel below.

She gasped in astonishment; overwhelmed and emotional. From first crossing the stream, she'd never witnessed so much beauty within one place. It was surreal!

Serge took hold of her hand. "Come with us, Eve. Let's walk the labyrinth."

The three of them approached the labyrinth and stopped beside the entrance. The Couture's labyrinth was not like other labyrinth. It was open and its path had been lovingly created by Serge's muscular hands. The glistening pieces of marble, shone brightly as the sun's rays caught sight of them, had been transformed into a spectacular mosaic walkway.

"You should state your intention now, Eve", prompted Suzette.

Eve looked puzzled. "I don't know what you mean."

"Just think of something that you want to achieve for yourself, or help for someone else. Then state that intention silently to yourself."

Now she understood. She silently did as she was told.

Serge entered the labyrinth first, slowly traversing forwards and backwards along the shimmering path until he reached the centre. He beckoned Eve to follow him. She sauntered along the straight lines, turning at each point until she reached him; taking in the magnificence of her surroundings as she went.

Both watched as Suzette commenced her own journey. Once she'd reached them, Serge beckoned them to sit, cross-legged, at each corner of the triangular sculpture. There were no other sounds except for the trickling water and the gentle, whooshing sound from the triangles.

"We'll sit here for a while. Close your eyes, Eve. Meditate on your intention and allow your mind to relax."

Closing her eyes, she could feel a calmness surrounding her body. Following several minutes of concentration, she began to see different shades of purple within her mind's eye. Swirling clouds wafted past her and she could feel herself going deeper into the meditation. The spiritual sensation was so subtle, that she hadn't recognised that she'd entered a higher state of being. Captivated by the feeling of floating across the sky amongst the clouds, her heart rate slowed even further and she felt very relaxed.

In her meditative state, she repeated her intention. "Please help me to achieve what I've come here to do."

After twenty minutes or so had passed, which only seemed like two to Eve, Serge brought them back from their meditative state, by asking them to open their eyes slowly and to take some time to become accustomed to their surroundings. Once fully aware, they each made their way back, in single file, to the entrance and as they stepped out of the labyrinth, Serge reminded them to offer up a silent 'thank you' for their experience.

"How do you feel, Eve?" Serge enquired, as they entered the summer house.

"I feel a tremendous sense of peace. This place is so tranquil, I could stay here forever. I felt as if I was slowly shifting into a deeper state of concentration. Clouds of several shades of purple surrounded me and floated in and out of my vision. I wanted to step into them and go with them."

Suzette moved closer towards Eve.

"Seeing colours in meditation is common. The different shades of purple are associated with your crown chakra and your third eye chakra, representing spirituality and enigma. It means that the colour you are seeing relates to the part of your body which requires healing. It is evoking your intuitive senses and may be related to the intention which you stated when you entered the labyrinth."

Eve waited before speaking, trying to take in what she was hearing. She knew that the part of her body which needed healing was her mind.

"My intention was to achieve what I came here to do and that was to rid myself of past issues and move on with my life."

Suzette chose a flattened piece of smooth amethyst that was energising within the large amethyst geode and placed it into the palm of Eve's hand. The amethyst crystal was to give her protection and the added strength to carry out her intention; she would need as much strength as she could gather to deal with what she was about to experience. Suzette also knew that once Eve had addressed her issues, she'd find peace; but she'd have to go through her own level of pain to reach it.

Serge listened. Eve's issues were not that dissimilar to his own problems.

"Shall we eat now", he asked.

They returned along the meditation path in

silence, each contemplating the recent event as they walked.

After a light lunch, washed down with several glasses of water, they went to their rooms to lie down.

Rest was essential after meditation; more so for Eve who'd entered into a deeper level of contemplation.

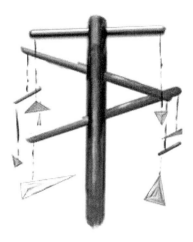

CHAPTER SIXTEEN

Gabriel arrived at 7pm prompt, bearing gifts; a case of 1531 Blanquette de Limoux and two bouquets of white roses; one for Eve and one for Suzette.

Eve had heard the taxi arrive and although she felt a little excited, she was also apprehensive. She'd purposely delayed getting ready and going downstairs before he arrived; she wanted to catch a glimpse of him through her bedroom window. The vision she saw did not disappoint!

Her eyes feasted on a tall, slim man with close-cropped grey hair. Dressed in slim-fitting, black jeans and a pure-white shirt, open at the neck and rolled up at the sleeves, he oozed class. Highly-polished black leather shoes and a pale lemon, v-neck sweater tied around his shoulders completed his quintessential ensemble.

She sneaked a last look in the mirror, flicked her fingers through her shoulder-length brown hair and made her way downstairs.

Gabriel was waiting for her at the bottom of the stairs. He handed her the roses and kissed her on both cheeks.

"Bonjour Eve. I am pleased to meet you."

"Bonjour Gabriel. I am pleased to meet you too. Thank you. The roses are beautiful."

She smiled nervously and took the roses into the kitchen to put them into a vase.

"Well, Madame. Is Gabriel to your liking?" asked Suzette.

The only answer that was forthcoming was, "I need a drink. A large one!"

Eve had deduced that Gabriel was wearing Tom Ford, Private Blend, Neroli Portofino. She was wearing it too. Such impeccable taste!

She returned to the dining area and took a seat opposite Gabriel. Serge was busy pouring Limoux into crystal glasses.

"I presume this is where I sit?" she asked Serge.

"Yes, of course it is. I've seated you opposite Gabriel. I'm sure you'll both have lots to talk about."

Suzette came out of the kitchen and Serge

handed out the glasses of chilled Limoux.

"Here's to a wonderful evening", Serge announced.

After chinking of glasses, Serge and Suzette returned to the kitchen to complete the finishing touches to the starter.

Eve was sure she'd have a wonderful evening; but she was not too sure about her health at this moment. She felt flushed and her mental agility was being tested as she struggled to speak coherently. Never mind, if she fainted, there *was* a doctor in the house!

"So, Eve. What line of work are you in?" His crisp pronunciation surprised her and yet she could still hear the seductive French undertones beneath his excellent diction.

She took another sip of wine and breathed deeply before answering.

"I'm in interior design. I travel between England and southern Spain mostly. My last three commissions have been in Malaga."

"How interesting. I'd like to hear more."

At that moment, a caramelised, French onion tartlet with goat's cheese and rosemary was placed in front of Eve and Gabriel. Suzette and Serge took their place at the table.

"Bon repas", announced Suzette.

She watched, in anticipation, to see the expressions on her guests' faces as they tucked in to the starter. She'd added a generous amount of parmesan and a pinch of cayenne pepper to the pastry mix to give it a cheesy flavour. Lovingly, she had gently cooked the onions in melted butter until they'd turned a golden-caramel colour and then she'd carefully shaped the pliable, goat's cheese into small circles , so that they'd fit evenly in the centre, on top of the onion mixture.

Gabriel cut into his tart and placed a small amount onto his fork. Placing the portion into his mouth, the sweetness of the caramelised onions juxtaposed with the strong-tasting goat's cheese, set his taste buds tingling. The sharpness of the miniscule side dressing of rocket infused with balsamic and lime, added to his bliss. He licked his lips to remove any trace of balsamic and caught Eve watching him. Flirtingly, he grinned at her and she pursed her lips, also in appreciation of the magnificent delicacy placed before her.

"This is my favourite starter, Suzette", Eve enthused.

"It's delicious", echoed Gabriel.

Suzette beamed as Serge piped in. "You can see what I think, ma chérie . My plate is nearly empty."

When they'd finished eating, Suzette and Serge cleared the table and went into the kitchen.

To cleanse their palates, Suzette served an elderflower and lemon sorbet to Eve and Gabriel. She and Serge ate theirs whilst in the kitchen. They wanted to give their guests some time alone to get to know each other.

"How about you, Gabriel? I know that you

are a doctor, but tell me a little about you and your interests?" Eve asked in between spoonfuls of the citrusy sorbet.

"Ok, where do I begin? I'm sixty-five in December. I've been married once and have had two, or maybe three, long term relationships. They didn't work out. I have a beautiful daughter who is twenty-five and a beautiful granddaughter, who is ten months old. I like to read. I'm quite a good singer. I like to travel. Is that enough for now?"

Serge came in and topped up their glasses. Without saying a word, he returned to the kitchen.

Eve was beginning to relax. She was having a glorious time.

"I've been married twice, though I'm not married now. I have a son who is thirty-eight this year and a grandson who is ten. I can't divulge my age though; it is a lady's prerogative, you know", she chuckled.

Gabriel, mentally calculated her age as being similar to his, or thereabouts!

"I haven't always been in design. I used to work as a Marketing Director for a reputable manufacturing organisation but, after thirty years of doing the 'same old same', I decided to take early retirement and train for a different career in design. It's the best thing I've ever done. I've travelled to several countries and I've met some interesting people. I love my job."

Serge and Suzette returned to the table carrying four plates. At one end of each white, oblong server, a perfect oblong portion of sea bass perched elegantly on a narrow bed of sautéed wild mushrooms. Three seared asparagus tips and a miniscule brunoise of diced ratatouille were arranged artistically at the other end.

They ate in moderate silence, except for sighs of appreciation, until their plates were empty. The cuisine deserved respect, as did the hosts.

The remainder of their evening was filled with much noteworthy conversation, whilst eating the dessert and nibbling a variety of cheeses from the cheese platter.

At twelve o'clock, Gabriel's taxi arrived. He needed to sleep in readiness for the day ahead. He didn't really know what to expect, but he was open to new experiences; in more ways than one!

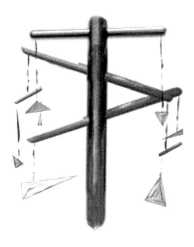

CHAPTER SEVENTEEN

Suzette arose early. She wanted to prepare herself for the day ahead. The course was to be held inside the clearing, surrounded by the labyrinth and the oscillating triangles. It was the perfect setting.

After showering she put on some loose, linen trousers and a multi-coloured shirt; tying a scarf, turban-style, around her head.

Sauntering along the meditation path, she wondered what the day would bring.

She sat in the summer house, reflecting on her own journey of discovery. It had, at times, been fraught with challenging disappointments, heartaches and hurt, but she knew that it was important for her to have had those experiences. They were part of her spiritual evolution. Quietly, she absorbed her surroundings. This area had a such a calming effect on her.

Aware that negative energies were likely to be dispersed later, she would need to protect and ground herself. She couldn't risk endangering her own wellbeing, as she would need all her energy to support the group. Just because she was spiritually advanced, she knew that her enlightenment would not provide automatic protection.

Suzette found a suitable place in between the labyrinth and the oscillating sculpture so she could ground herself. Standing upright, with her feet apart to balance herself, she vertically aligned her backbone before stretching her arms upwards. Visualising herself as a mature tree, she imagined her roots penetrating deeply into the ground, soaking up the earth's natural energy.

Bringing her arms down slightly, she outstretched them to her side and asked for her spirit guide, Broken Feather, to protect her. As an extra protection, she encased herself in a cloak of white light and whispered her usual prayer.

"Help me to do your work, God. Help me to be of service to others."

After the grounding process, she traversed the labyrinth and sat for a while in meditation, before returning to the summer house to check that all was ready for the course later.

Serge had already transferred the garden furniture from the pool area and he'd sited it in a shady area under the walnut trees. Satisfied with the preparations, Suzette returned to the house. Serge had left a note saying that he had gone to visit Nicole and Hugo with some fresh provisions.

As she prepared breakfast, she could hear Eve singing in the shower. Gabriel was expected at ten and Suzette was eager to start on time. There was a lot to cover in the first two sessions.

Still singing, Eve entered the kitchen and hugged Suzette.

"Morning, Suzette. Did you sleep well?"

Yes, thanks. Did you?"

"Not really. I was tossing and turning. I was thinking about the course and what it entails."

Suzette grinned as she continued arranging the breakfast on the serving plates.

"I guess you like him, then?"

Eve raised her eyebrows, feigning surprise at Suzette's question. She nodded.

"I may do!"

They both carried the breakfast onto the kitchen terrace and waited for Serge to return.

Eve indulged herself in several cups of coffee, whilst Suzette sipped peppermint infusion.

Footsteps on the gravel alerted them to Serge's arrival.

"Bonjour, beautiful ladies. Are you well?"

"Bonjour", they replied in unison.

Over a hearty breakfast, they sensitively

discussed Nicole's deteriorating health and Suzette shrewdly evaded answering questions about the course. She didn't want to reveal too much and made an excuse to clear the breakfast dishes.

On hearing a car pull up on the driveway, Suzette went outside to greet Gabriel. As she walked past Eve's chair, she could see that she was flustered and blushing. Putting her arm around her friend, she whispered "Breathe in, breathe out."

Gabriel smiled as he confidently strode towards them.

"Bonjour, my friends."

He embraced Suzette and Serge before kissing Eve on her cheeks, whilst grasping her hand.

"Serge, Gabriel. Could you carry the water and the fruit for me please? I'll just lock up and then we 'll be ready to go.

Gabriel wondered where they were going as they made their way across the stream and along the meditation path. He hadn't ventured into this part of the garden before. The tranquillity was palpable and he immediately felt a calming sensation as he followed Serge into the clearing. His eyes widened in surprise as he gaped at the surreal surroundings in front of him. Speechless, he allowed himself to become engrossed in the confines of this hidden sanctuary.

"I never imagined this", he whispered.

Suzette guided them towards the table and beckoned them to sit. She poured water into glasses and placed the bowl of fruit onto the table.

"Firstly, Gabriel, let me welcome you to the clearing. Eve has already experienced its beauty for the first time yesterday, so she does have an awareness of it."

Eve nodded in acknowledgement.

"Serge, would you like to explain to Eve and Gabriel about how our private sanctuary came into fruition?"

"Yes. I'll gladly do so."

He rearranged the position of his chair and made himself comfortable.

"After I'd asked Suzette to become my wife, I knew that I wanted to give her something that she would treasure for a wedding present. The clearing provided a great opportunity for me to design a place where she could fully embrace her need for solitude and contemplation."

Serge locked eyes with Suzette and she smiled in admiration for the words he'd just spoken.

"I knew that triangles featured strongly in her life. Triangles are deemed to be the strongest geometric shape and Suzette is a strong woman. Her unique jewellery and many of her designs also have triangular aspects; as does her belief in the past, present and future."

Eve nodded in agreement. She'd always been intrigued with Suzette's fascination for everything triangular.

Gabriel listened intently as Serge continued.

"I specifically designed the meditation path,

the labyrinth and the fountain to incorporate Suzette's magnetic compulsion with the three-sided shape. In truth, I must also admit that I was also fulfilling my own desire to construct an irregular piece of art; one which I knew she'd appreciate."

He was silent for a moment as he turned towards the labyrinth.

"I worked in solitude, forbidding Suzette to cross the stream. For several months I took great pleasure in transforming the space. For me, it was a therapeutic and rewarding experience. I loved every minute."

Gabriel interrupted.

"Suzette, were you not intrigued as to what he was doing?"

"I respected his wishes and his own need for privacy. I had an inkling that he was working on something for me. I was working on something for him at the same time. On occasions, I could see him taking delivery of building materials, but I made myself scarce, not wanting to betray his trust in me."

"Did you design the moving sculpture as well, Serge?" Gabriel questioned further.

"No. That was Suzette's wedding present to me."

Shaking his head in admiration, he raised his shoulders; unable to grasp what he was hearing.

Suzette walked over to the sculpture and

stood by it. It towered above her.

"After much contemplation, I decided that I would design a moving sculpture for Serge; one that would depict the ebb and flow of life. I wanted the triangles to look as if they were dancing freely in the air and sometimes kissing each other when the wind blew stronger. Love was the main theme for my piece of work. Love for my husband, love for my art and how the sculpture depicts the freedom to move and, love for myself and my ability to be the person I am."

Eve and Gabriel turned towards each other and gazed in amazement at her interpretation.

"I spent quite a bit of time trying to get the balance right. Once I was satisfied, I engaged the skilled services of a local engineering company to construct it for me. They were reluctant at first to take on the commission, but I persuaded them and on completion they were thrilled with the result; as I was."

Serge spied his chance to continue.

"I decided to name the sculpture, Oscillate. Oscillation is ever present in our lives. Changes occur whether we like it nor not. Nature oscillates with each season. The moving triangles reflect the movements of the leaves and branches of the trees, blowing in the surrounding orchard. I considered the name to be apt."

Suzette poured more water into the glasses and allowed a period of quietness before she continued.

"I'll now give you a brief introduction to the course and what it entails. Over the next five days we'll look at self-actualisation and how we can implement certain techniques into our daily lives, to improve our wellbeing."

After distributing some handouts explaining the concept of self-actualisation, she invited the group to comment.

After a short discussion, she handed Serge, Eve and Gabriel a pen, an envelope and a sheet of paper. At the top of the paper was a heading – Where am I now?

"Consider where you are at this moment in time in your lives. Just start writing and let your thoughts flow onto the paper. Keep writing for as long as you can. Once you've finished, place your writing in your envelope, seal it and put your name on it."

Suzette left them scribbling and walked back to the house, collecting several types of green leaves along the way. She'd use them in the mixed salad for lunch.

Whilst preparing the salad, she poured herself some elderflower presse which she made the previous week. It was a refreshing change to water and peppermint infusion. She would take some for the others to drink later.

She placed the baby chard, spinach leaves, Romaine lettuce, rocket and herbs into a large glass bowl and mixed them together. Gathering several ingredients from her store cupboard, she placed some olive oil, balsamic vinegar, sugar, salt, pepper and a tablespoon of mustard into a glass vinegar bottle and shook it vigorously before tasting it.

Deciding that the salad dressing needed something extra, she sprinkled some dried basil into the mixture and shook it again.

Slicing the vegetable quiche into quarters, which she'd conveniently baked the previous day, she collected some plates and cutlery and placed everything, including some freshly-baked almond biscuits, into a picnic basket.

Serge, Eve and Gabriel were putting their writings in their envelopes as she returned to the clearing.

Over lunch, they discussed the morning's session, with Gabriel wanting further clarification on the content of the course.

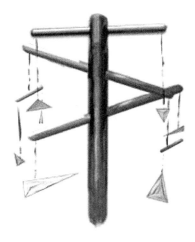

CHAPTER EIGHTEEN

After eating lunch, the group discussed the subject of enlightenment.

Suzette handed out three writing journals and instructed them to record any information or unusual occurrences which they may experience over the next few days. She also handed them two more pieces of paper and explained what was required of them.

"I want you to consider two things. Who are you and why are you here? I don't mean why are you here in this place now. I mean why are you here on earth?"

Serge was further along his spiritual path and knew the purpose of fulfilling the writing tasks.

Gabriel and Eve needed more explanation before they could put pen to paper.

"Open your minds. List the things relating to who you are – a mother, a father, a friend, a spirit in a human body. Then list the things relating to why you think you're here on earth. Think about it. What are you here for? Maybe you don't know why you're on this earth. Contemplate your answers and then write them down."

She placed a meditation CD in the player and went to sit inside the summer house; returning to the group once they'd their writing.

"Usually, at this point, I'd ask you to share your work with each other, if you want to. However, I think you'd al benefit from some meditation to calm your minds and your senses."

They all nodded in agreement. The writing tasks had stretched them mentally. Gabriel and Eve felt fatigued.

"Before we enter the labyrinth, I'm going to give you another piece of paper with an important question written on it. I know you're probably thinking 'not *more* writing'. This is your homework for the evening. Try to write at least two sides of A4 paper."

Sharing a glance of silent trepidation, they read the question. 'What do you really want out of your life?'

"Come now. You need to soothe your tired

minds. Let's walk the labyrinth."

Beside the entrance to the labyrinth, Serge stopped and spoke in a low voice.

Before we enter the labyrinth, I'd ask you firstly to state your intentions. Gabriel, think of something that you would like to achieve. It could be for yourself or you could ask for help for someone else. State this intention silently to yourself."

Gabriel nodded. He'd never experienced anything like this before. Neither had he come across the challenges of being asked to write about himself. The personal writing task had left him feeling quite vulnerable and emotional.

Serge guided the group into the labyrinth. Walking along the triangular-shaped marble path, it didn't take long before they arrived at the centre.

Although very intrigued as to what was happening, Gabriel was also apprehensive.

Suzette instructed everyone to sit around the triangle and make themselves comfortable.

"We'll sit here and allow our minds to relax. Close your eyes and listen to the gentle trickling of the water. Now, concentrate on your intentions and allow your anxious thoughts to float away. Take in several deep breaths and blow away those negative energies."

Eve was looking forward to the meditation. Nagging, negative reflections had surfaced when she'd been writing and she wanted to clear them from her mind.

Gabriel closed his eyes and tried to focus on his intention. It was difficult. He kept thinking of what he'd asked for and he wasn't sure whether it was achievable. "Allow me to forgive her and then I can move forward with my life", he repeated the words silently to himself.

After several minutes, he could feel himself relaxing. The image of his ex-wife came into his mind. He sensed the depth of his own anxiety as she told him that she was leaving him for another man. She was pregnant with the man's child. He re-lived the terror as she told him that she would be taking their daughter with her to live in England. The irony of it was that he hadn't even noticed that there were problems within his marriage.

The scene reverberated through his brain as he repeated, in his subconscious, the woeful words that had haunted him since she'd left him.

"No. You can't do this to me. No. No. No. She's my child too. No. This can't be happening."

He could see himself crying and begging her to stay. He was holding onto his daughter who was also crying. The pain was unbearable.

Serge's low voice distracted him from his tormented thoughts.

"Slowly open your eyes. Allow yourselves time to adjust to your surroundings."

Gabriel touched his cheek. His tears had been real; as real as the pain he had just re-lived.

"Take your time to adjust", Serge reassured them. He could see that Gabriel had been crying.

Eve had also experienced a similar type of turmoil and was surprised that this feeling had been different to her previous one the day before.

Conscious of what they had experienced, Suzette quickly reassured them both.

"This meditation was supposed to have had a calming effect on you both, but I can sense that it has awakened something deep within you. It does appear that you may have already commenced the clearing process. Sit awhile and take some deep breaths."

After leaving the labyrinth, the group sat around the table. Serge poured more water into their empty glasses and, in complete silence, they gathered their thoughts.

Suzette looked around the table at each of them. Whilst Serge seemed unperturbed, Eve and Gabriel's bewildered expressions were only to be expected. Their shoulders were slumped and Eve was trying to stifle a yawn.

Sensing a shift in energy, Suzette decided it was time to end the session.

"I can see that you've had a tiring day. Take your papers with you and keep them in your file. Don't forget to write in your journal if things come into your head. Please remember to complete the assignment I've given you and bring it with you tomorrow. It's an important part of the process."

Although Serge was already self-aware, the day had been tiring for him also. His mind had conjured up many past experiences when he'd been writing and he felt unsettled.

The day had been a demanding one for the group. Suzette discerned that the following day would also be equally as difficult; if not more so! The clearing process had commenced earlier than it usually did. It was within the third session that the most demanding task was tackled and clearing would take place.

By the time they arrived back at the house, it was 6.30pm. Exhausted, the group were void of speech.

After waving farewell to Gabriel, the others went inside.

Eve politely excused herself and went to her room. Collapsing on the bed, she reflected on the day's events. It hadn't been what she'd expected; although she hadn't really known what to expect! Her fears soon subsided as she permitted a serene sensation to penetrate her being and she drifted off into a deep sleep.

Downstairs, Serge had already commenced his writing. Suzette was in the kitchen preparing some sandwiches. They'd decided earlier that they wouldn't eat a hot meal.

Before going upstairs to Eve's bedroom, Suzette covered some sandwiches with a linen napkin and placed them and a jug of water onto a tray. The door was slightly ajar as she approached the room and she found Eve lying on top of the bed, fully dressed and fast asleep.

Suzette placed a cotton sheet over her and

set down the tray onto the side table before quietly closing the door.

As she entered the living area, she could see that Serge was totally engrossed in his writing. Several sheets of paper were strewn on the floor at the side of him and a half-eaten sandwich was left on his plate. She refilled his glass with water and left him to it.

Sitting at the dining table, Suzette ate her sandwich and pondered over earlier events. The group had been responsive from the start and many hidden emotions had been disturbed during the process. They were all mentally drained.

****

In the next village, Gabriel had also taken to his bed. He was exhausted, had a headache and he felt shaky and tired. Sleep had evaded him for several years now. His human circadian-rhythm was out of balance and he found it difficult to stay asleep for more than four hours at a time. He'd nap in the afternoon to catch up on his sleep, but he always felt tired.

He reflected on his recent experience in the labyrinth; aware that he'd concealed his problem for many years. When his ex-wife had left, it was easier to allow his daughter to go to England, than going through the courts. He couldn't bear to see his precious daughter suffer any more than she had to. He didn't want her to see his anger and his pain. He'd provided for his daughter in monetary terms, taken her on holiday several times a year and telephoned her three or four times a week. If he was honest with himself, the profound sorrow that he felt in 'losing' his daughter was far worse than the heartache he felt in losing his wife to another man.

He picked up the pen and the words flowed effortlessly onto the sheets of paper. The day had awakened something within him. It wasn't a pleasant awakening by any means; it was a totally unexpected one. Focusing on his writing, he dared not think of what tomorrow would bring.

****

Eve had slept soundly until the early hours. Reaching over, she switched on the light and was pleased to see that Suzette had left sandwiches and a drink.

After satisfying her hunger and her thirst, she remembered that she had to complete some writing. She stepped out of bed and retrieved the file from the dressing table.

Opening it, a piece of paper with a heading 'What do you really want out of your life?' stared back at her. She knew what she wanted, but she didn't know whether it was attainable.

Putting pen to paper, she started to write. After completing four sides of paper, she inserted her writing into the file, took off her clothes and climbed back into bed.

Within five minutes, she was asleep again.

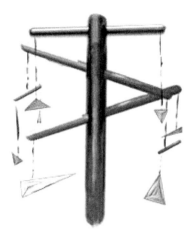

CHAPTER NINETEEN

Files in hands, the group assembled in the clearing. Lavender oil was smouldering in a ceramic burner on the table whilst serene murmurs of meditation music drifted from inside the summer house.

"Today is going to be demanding for you all. You'll complete a free association task and then you'll start to think about clearing past issues. This afternoon, we'll discuss human oscillation and the effects of absorbing negative energies."

Apprehensively, the group gazed at each other across the table.

"Would any of you like to share what you've

written? It's not compulsory that you share, but it can have a releasing effect on your concealed pent-up emotions," Suzette explained.

Eve and Gabriel declined the offer. Serge took several deep breaths.

"I'll share my writing with you. What I really want out of my life is to rid myself of the painful memories which imprison me. I want to be able to feel a sense of freedom and peace. I want to be free of the back pain which prevents me from living an active life. Moreover, I want to rid myself of the feelings of depression that creep upon me unawares and hold me captive. I want to feel well again in my body and in my mind."

Serge stopped speaking for a moment to compose himself.

I've written several pages, but I won't bore you reading them all."

Acknowledging her husband's contribution, she smiled reassuringly.

"Thank you, Serge. Anyone else?"

Eve and Gabriel remained silent, shaking their heads. They weren't ready to share.

"Ok. We'll now go straight into the free association task. I'd like you to access your unconscious mind and allow it to run free. Write down any type of random words or thoughts that come into your minds. They may not make any sense to you, but write them down anyway. Listen to the music and try to relax."

Suzette observed their reactions.

Serge's pen furiously navigated the blank sheet of white paper. He scribbled the word LOSS in capital letters at the top of the page and, without any hesitation, he immediately made a list of bullet points.

LOSS

- Francesca
- unborn babies and the chance to become a father
- time lost creating sculptures instead of spending precious time with my sick wife – not wanting to accept her imminent death!
- self-respect – drinking too much
- self
- sanity challenged
- Maman and père to dementia
- dignity
- time wasted by not facing up to issues.

LOSS
LOSS
LOSS
LOSS

At the other end of the table, Gabriel had also started scribbling. In the middle of the page he'd written his name in a circle and underlined it several times. He filled the page with masses of words; all in capital letters.

Seeing the other two writing furiously, Eve started to write, also filling her page with words and phrases.

Whilst the group had been writing, Suzette walked the labyrinth. In contemplation, she'd asked for help for all of them. She also gave thanks for everything she had in her life. She was grateful for her husband, her precious family, her friends, her lifestyle and her health. She was grateful that she'd been given the opportunities to help others along their paths. She knew it was her birth mission.

Re-tracing her steps, she walked slowly out of the labyrinth and back to the others. They'd finished writing and were chatting.

"Are you ready for some lunch?" Suzette asked.

They all nodded.

Suzette strolled along the meditation path, crossed the pebbled stream and walked towards the house. She could sense that there was a shift in energy and attitude within the group.

CHAPTER TWENTY

As the engaging triangles oscillated in a slow hypnotic motion, Suzette likened the backward and forward movements to the way in which the group also oscillated between their own compulsions to hold onto something that they'd been nurturing for years and, the desperate craving of wanting to free themselves from their pain and suffering at the same time.

Suzette was clairsensitive. She could sense the anxiety emanating from the group and their reluctance to move forward. She'd need to remain firm in her resolute if she were to deliver the intensive programme within the time constraints; the aim being that the group would make swift changes.

Waiting for a break in their conversation, she spoke.

"Let me help you to make sense of what you're experiencing at the moment. Take a look at Oscillate. When the wind is calm, the triangles move freely and gently; to and fro, back and forth. They are now in balance. When there is a stronger, more forceful wind, that's when friction occurs and the triangles move frantically; trying their best to regain their balance. When the wind has blown through and moved on, the triangles regain their balance and equilibrium reigns once more."

Mesmerised, they watched the triangles, swaying back and forth in harmony.

Suzette recognised the calming effect that the oscillating sculpture was having on them and she continued with her explanation.

"Oscillation is taking place within all of you now. The winds of change are blowing, displacing your feelings and forcing you to make some very important decisions. In essence, you've all been oscillating for many years, frequently repeating your daily, harmful patterns of repressing your true feelings. You've been reluctant to change your regular habits and those self-limiting patterns have affected your well-being."

Remaining silent, she allowed the group to digest her comments. The pain, etched in their furrowed brows and their anguished expressions, revealed their inner turmoil and sadness.

"When friction happens within our lives, it upsets our equilibrium. Our body rhythms are disrupted and therefore we become vulnerable. Our emotions are more extreme and intense. Our behaviour is affected. In order to survive, we bury our emotions deep within us and nourish them by thinking about them constantly. In our attempts to analyse the reasons why things have happened, we keep going over those thoughts again and again. We don't realise the consequences of holding onto our negative experiences. In doing so, we are only strengthening the bond and the self-inflicted pain persists."

All three were deeply emotional. Tightly, they held onto each other's hands and then they stood up and hugged each other.

Eve wiped her eyes with the back of her hand and sat down again, before sharing her own philosophy.

"If we think about what's happening to us now, we're all in the same boat; pushing our oars backwards and forwards, trying to survive the storm which rages within us. We push harder and harder against the tide, trying to hold onto the belief that if we keep on doing what we are doing, in time the storm will subside and go away. What we don't realise is that the more we push against the natural flow of our bodies, which is trying to reject the toxic energies, the more our energies will be depleted by our resistance."

Serge and Gabriel nodded and smiled at her, encouraging her to continue.

"I can see now that by holding onto my self-destructing memories, I'll remain in exactly the same place, unable to move forward. I'll just keep doing the same as I've always done — feeding my negative energies by revisiting my memories and I'll keep getting what I've always got; heartache, pain, anxiety and feelings of depression."

Tearful again, she stopped for a moment to compose herself.

"Perhaps we've all been pushing in the wrong direction for too long. Maybe, instead of resisting, if we go with the flow, the boat will take us in the direction we want to go in. Maybe we need to discover new ways to project ourselves forward. Maybe, the friction in our lives occurred to teach us something. Who knows? Instead of resisting the shift, maybe we should embrace it."

Serge nodded. "Well executed, Eve. I am, most definitely, in the same boat as you. I've been paddling my oars in the wrong direction for many years and getting nowhere fast!"

Gabriel laughed. "Me too. Over the years I've worn out many oars whilst I've been pushing hard against the tide."

He gazed affectionately at Eve, admiring the way she articulately explained the situation that they all found themselves in. He'd noticed many qualities in her since he'd met her; qualities which he respected and liked.

Eve caught his gaze and smiled. There were several commonalities in their lives, which she thought could be nurtured into something special.

Maybe, they could heal each other!

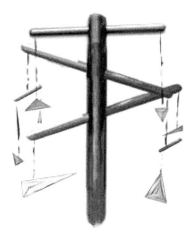

CHAPTER TWENTY ONE

Day three of the course brought more challenges for the group.

After sharing their notes from their journals, Serge, Eve and Gabriel could recognize each other's emerging, positive thought-patterns. There were commonalities between what had been written.

Suzette informed them of what was going to be the content of the session.

"Today, we're going to discuss several topics. We'll look at victim consciousness and the power of thought. We'll also look at control dramas and forgiveness. Finally, you'll decide on the changes you want to make in your lives."

The three participants glanced at each other and raised their eyebrows. What next?

Suzette had decided she'd drip-feed their curiosity. She wanted them to absorb the lessons and information-overload was not on the menu.

"Firstly, can I ask if anyone here feels that they are a victim of circumstance?"

Gabriel was quick to answer.

"I do. I feel rejected and abandoned by those people who I thought loved me – or should have loved me! I wanted my parents' love as a child, but didn't receive it. I worked hard to provide a good lifestyle for my wife and daughter, but they left me. My sanity was challenged. I felt vulnerable and fragile."

Suzette nodded, acknowledging his reply.

"Eve, do you feel as if you are a victim?"

"Yes. I, very much, feel like I'm a victim. I was controlled by my parents, my family, my husbands and partners; even my friends and work colleagues thought that they had to have a say in my life. I rebelled against societal expectations, feeling very confused, hurt, rejected and angry. Yes. Definitely. I'm a victim of their cruel actions. I often ask why did it have to happen to me!"

"Thanks, Eve."

Suzette looked towards Serge was sitting.

"I, too, feel like a victim. I feel that the loss I have endured throughout my life has turned me into a victim. I feel so sorry for myself at times. I didn't want those things to happen, but they did."

Suzette gave them a little time to reflect.

"Being a victim strips your positive energy levels. Allowing yourself to become a victim is a damaging approach to the way you live. Your self-destructing thought-patterns control the way you behave and distort your rational thinking."

Sensing that the group were finding it difficult to accept her theory, she took a different stance. Maybe, they'd been victims for so long, they'd become comfortable with the 'label'.

"Just allow yourself feel your vulnerabilities and your fears. Then, try to release any blame from yourself and from other people. By doing this, you're releasing any control that you think they may have over you."

She went on to explain in more detail about control dramas, positive and negative energies and forgiveness.

"When we talk about forgiving, it's not the same as forgetting. You may feel as if you can't forgive the person for the harmful events that have occurred within your lives. If you can recognise that forgiveness is a learning curve and, if you have the intention to forgive at this moment, then forgiveness will happen in time."

Eve interrupted.

"Are you suggesting that by not forgiving, it's preventing us from living a fuller life? Are you saying that if we allow others to control us, that it's our fault?"

"I think you'll all know the answers to Eve's questions. Reflect on your experiences and you'll come up with your own answers."

Leaving the group to ponder further, Suzette returned to the house to collect lunch.

CHAPTER TWENTY TWO

After feasting on a lunch of Caesar salad, fresh fruit and nuts, they continued with the session.

Suzette explained the value of positive self-talk and the possibility of changing negative habits.

"Some of the negative habits which we possess are learnt from our parents, our family and even our friends. This 'learned behaviour' becomes the 'norm' and part of our everyday life."

Gabriel rested his hand on his chin.

" I totally agree with what you are saying, Suzette. We conform with the culture, so that we 'fit in'; not wanting to be perceived as being any different from others. I was like that when I was younger. I didn't agree with others' points of view, but I was too scared to disagree. It was only as I got older that I felt confident enough to challenge."

Suzette continued.

"The next task is to decide on the changes you want to make. You may only choose to make one change to begin with; or you might want to make a few small changes. Whatever you decide, those changes need to be actioned immediately. If you attempt to procrastinate, the changes will not occur. Take some time to think about the changes. Go and find a place where you can sit alone and write down your decisions in your journals."

The group dispersed. Serge walked over to the labyrinth, Eve entered the summer house and Gabriel sat beneath the oscillating triangles.

Suzette stayed at the table and awaited their return.

Approximately thirty minutes later, the group returned to their seats.

"So, have you all decided on your changes? Would you like to share your decisions?"

"I would", Eve offered. "Later, I'm going to telephone my family and my friends. I'll talk with them about how they made me feel when they treated me unkindly. I won't talk with my parents; they are too frail to understand what I want to convey. Neither will I confront my ex-husbands. I've made a decision to forgive them all. It would be futile not to! I'm going to make the calls later.

It's time I moved on with my life."

She sighed. Her lips quivered, as she realised that the task ahead of her would be challenging; to say the least.

Gesturing their full support, Serge and Gabriel took hold of her hands and gripped them tightly.

"I, too, am going to make contact with my wife and my daughter to let them know exactly how I felt when they left. I've decided to forgive my wife for what happened. I can't change what happened, but I can certainly learn from those events. I'm looking forward to manifesting my future and clearing the stuff I've been nurturing for years."

He looked over at Eve. He had a strong feeling that she would feature in his future.

Hands still clasped with Eve and Gabriel, it was now Serge's turn to share his decision.

"When I was in the labyrinth, my inner voice spoke to me. It encouraged me to let go of my self-restricting thoughts, instead of topping them up with new ones. I know that my intuition guided me to where I am now in my life. I understand now that life is about phases of suffering and happiness; and all other kinds of emotions and obstacles."

He stopped for a moment to compose himself. His emotions were seizing his words, preventing him from speaking.

"I've forgiven myself for feeling the way I

did. Francesca and my parents were constants in my life. They bestowed so much love on me and they supported me in my work. I acknowledge that there was meaning to my suffering. I know that Francesca and my parents were grateful for the way I cared for them; they told me, many times."

Suzette began to send him some energy. She could sense he was struggling.

"I know now, that it's just one of my purposes in life to care for people. My pain and my loss have enabled me to understand Hugo and the traumas he has endured in his life – and another trauma he'll soon have to endure. I'll take care of him throughout and after his forthcoming loss."

Suzette, proud of her husband's admissions, had great difficulty holding back her own emotions.

"Thank you all, for sharing your decisions. I think we've had enough for one day, don't you?"

All nodding in agreement, they gathered up their belongings and the four of them walked in silence along the winding path and back towards the house.

Gabriel bid his farewell and left. He had to prepare himself before making the telephone calls. It wouldn't be easy.

Eve also had calls to make. She felt strong enough to confront her fears and speak to the people whom she'd allowed to control her!

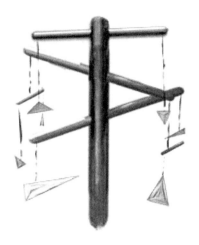

CHAPTER TWENTY THREE

The previous evening had been one of liberation for Eve and for Gabriel. Telephone calls had been made, important and civil words had been spoken and positive energy levels were raised. It was evident that self-actualisation was taking place.

Within the clearing, session four had already commenced and there was an air of optimistic enthusiasm spiralling around the participants.

Suzette could see their auras as they chatted, enthusiastically, about the empowering changes which had taken place over the last few days.

Serge's aura was gold in colour; indicating that a renewed spiritual energy was present. Gold also signified possessing a strong and philosophical connection with knowing oneself.

Suzette had immediately sensed his increased vibrations last evening when they'd discussed the progress he had made whilst in bed. She'd pleasantly experienced a renewed physical energy in him too!

A pink aura was visible around Eve's head and shoulders; showing a purity of intention and the revealing of a recent love interest. When pink is in a person's aura, it indicates a strong attraction to the arts and to nature's beauty. How apt! Suzette was aware of the magnetic intenseness of Eve and Gabriel's evolving relationship.

Within Gabriel's human energy field, a blue aura was evident. The colour blue is related to the throat chakra and represents verbal clarity and a distinct expression of one's thoughts and feelings. Suzette imagined him speaking honestly to his wife and daughter and forgiving them. He emanated vitality, juxtaposed with an innate calmness.

Observing them all speaking animatedly about the effects the course had bestowed on them, she felt certain that the winds of change, once again, were blowing in their direction.

There was no need for further facilitation or to elicit more information from them. They were healing each other with descriptions of their own advancement.

Serge proffered information about his recent personal growth.

"My intrusive, mind-chattering is no longer in residence. My back pain is hardly noticeable. I think that the combination of everything that has transpired lately and being with you all, has had a powerful impact on my psyche. I've experienced an awakening. My wife's dedication to her work and her patient, yet persistent, approach in delivering this course has enabled this change to occur within me."

"Thank you for those thoughtful words, Serge. I only facilitated the change. All of you have worked very hard to make your own changes happen. It is you who have cleared your own negative energies, when you completed the free association task. You decided on those changes and then you manifested those changes. You now have a clearer vision of where you are in your lives and what you want to do with your lives."

Eve reiterated Serge's words.

"Suzette, you've taught me how to listen more intently to my intuition and to follow it. You've encouraged me to be selective about who I want to spend time with; by removing superfluous people from my life. You've equally inspired me by urging me to believe in myself and be the person I want to be and am; not allowing others to control me. I can't thank you enough."

Gabriel waited patiently for Eve to finish

speaking before he relayed his views.

"I feel so different this morning. I feel alive and excited about what's ahead of me. When you used the phrase 'live your own life and let others live theirs', I now understand what you meant. I have no control whatsoever over anyone's life and neither would I want someone to control my life. I can't live their life. I can only live my own."

Pausing for a moment, he reflected on his past habits.

"The self-attacking inner critic within me had become a familiar part of me, constantly nagging away at me and judging me at every opportune moment. I'm going to have a clear-out and get rid of objects that remind me of my ex-wife and all those negative events that keep me from moving forward."

Eve smiled at him and admired his spirit.

"I intend living my life to the fullest. I made another significant decision last night. Retirement and adventure awaits me. I am going to deliver my resignation on Monday. Thank you, Suzette, for giving me the tools to become more self-aware and for helping me to recognise how I've wasted my life, whilst I was dwelling on what should or could have been."

"Nothing is wasted, Gabriel. The many facets of life which you've experienced have allowed you to discern the difference between extreme sadness and true happiness. It's a part of your life which cannot be erased; nor should it be.

It was meant to be!"

"You think so, Suzette?"

"I know so, Gabriel."

They'd completed the course within four days. An intensive course is usually of five days' duration, but Serge, Eve and Gabriel had fully embraced the tasks and acted swiftly on them.

"After lunch, we'll complete the final task and an evaluation of the course. We've managed to do everything within four days, so I think you can have tomorrow off. Spend the day doing whatever pleases you most. Now, talk amongst yourselves whilst I collect the food."

On returning with the lunch, she couldn't help but think that the 'unfreezing, change and re-freezing' process had been successful in bringing about an instantaneous transformation.

They'd all found the courage to step outside their comfort zone. They were about to step into another zone; a zone which would expand their spiritual awareness and take them a step further on their self-actualised journey.

CHAPTER TWENTY FOUR

Suzette handed out three sheets of lined paper. The title on top of the page read 'Where am I now?'

"As you did at the start of the course, I'd like you to slowly reflect on the last four days and consider where you are, at this moment in time."

No sooner had she finished speaking, the three of them started to write; pens furiously gliding over the white sheets, as if they were frightened they would forget what they wanted to write.

Suzette observed the oscillating triangles moving, rhythmically, back and forth and she resonated with how they'd all regained their equilibrium. She believed that Oscillate had played an important part in their healing, as had the labyrinth, the meditation path and the abundance of nature that resided within and around the outskirts of the clearing.

She waited for them to finish their writing before she handed them their sealed envelopes. Four days ago, they had penned words of woe. Today, she would watch their expressions as they each compared their own pieces of text.

"Here are your envelopes. Open them now and compare the words you've written on both occasions."

Ripping open their envelopes, they scoured the contents.

"I can't believe it", exclaimed Gabriel. I've come so far in such a short amount of time. On Monday I was a desperate soul. I blamed others for the way I felt. I questioned why things had happened to me. I had regrets. I was angry and I felt rejected."

He glanced at the words he'd just written.

"Today, I feel empowered. I've forgiven my wife, my daughter and my family for the way my life emerged. I'm so happy with who I am now. I've created a vision for my future and I'm calm and enlightened."

Suzette, Eve and Serge smiled.

"My turn", Eve announced. Shaking her head, she raised her eyebrows at the words which were displayed on the page in front of her.

"On Monday I, also, was in an undesirable place. I had very little energy and I felt depressed and hurt at the thought of regurgitating past issues; issues that were making me unwell, both physically and mentally. Today, I'm a transformed woman. How could I have changed so drastically within a matter of days? I've forgiven and moved on. I realised that last evening. I feel a lightness of spirit and a grateful appreciation of the liberation that my clearness of mind has given me. I'm really excited about what lies ahead of me."

She paused for a few moments before continuing.

"I've also learned that the mind can heal, or it can destroy. I will not let it destroy me."

"That's good to hear, Eve. I see that you and Gabriel have used the same word – forgiveness. Forgiving has freed you both from energy-draining thoughts."

They both nodded in agreement.

"Serge, what differences did you notice?"

"The word LOSS featured strongly within my first piece of writing. The word GAIN is the key focus of my writing today. Through my loss, I've gained so much. I've gained a beautiful wife and a welcome release from the physical back pain which I've endured for many, many years. I've spiritually transcended and I know that I'm a much stronger person; strong enough to be of service to those who need help. My creativity is heightened and

I'm ready to start a new project; although my intuition is telling me that the time is not yet right."

Her husband's words were pleasing to hear.

"You've all transformed your own negative experiences into positive ones. You've converted loss into gain. Serge, I know you were already enlightened, but your deeply-ingrained sadness prevented you from growing. I'm so happy to hear that your back pain has subsided."

She glanced in Gabriel's direction He knew exactly what she was referring to.

"Complete the feedback sheets for me, please. They will be useful for me when I'm preparing my next course."

Whilst waiting for them to finish writing, she tidied the area.

"Gabriel, would you like to join us this evening for a celebratory dinner?"

"I'd be very honoured to accept your kind invitation, Madame Couture."

"Seven o'clock ok?"

"Seven is good for me. I look forward to it."

Once more they all trod the meditation path. Gabriel got into his car and drove off; excited at the prospect of being in Eve's company again.

He could hardly wait!

CHAPTER TWENTY FIVE

After eating breakfast, where last evening's meal was discussed in length by Eve, armed with writing paper and pens, a large bottle of water and some fruit, Suzette made her way over to her sanctuary. The hermit creature which resided comfortably within her, craved solitude.

Serge also took refuge in his studio.

After completion of the course, Suzette had felt the urgent need to re-energise. Although she'd protected herself each day from negative energies, delivering the course had been quite demanding.

On arriving at the clearing, she went into

the summer house and placed her writing tools on the table. She then walked over to her sculpture to prepare herself for meditation. The oscillating triangles swayed gently as she worked through several stretching exercises, whilst taking deep breaths.

Moving over to the labyrinth, she stated her intention at the entrance before traversing slowly along the straight lines until she arrived at the centre.

The trickling sound of the water from the fountain soothed her. Sitting upright and cross-legged, she closed her eyes and focused on her breathing. Clouds of bright green and vivid purple drifted effortlessly in front of her closed eyelids. She understood that this mental, spiritual discipline would gradually coax her mind and her body into a relaxing, peaceful state. Letting her thoughts flow freely, she could feel herself entering a deeper state of consciousness.

She sensed a spiritual presence. The fragrant perfume was unmistakable. It was Francesca.

The message came to her, loud and clear.

"Thank you for healing him, Suzette. He has been a troubled soul for a long time, even though he hides it well. This morning, I've witnessed a difference in his energy levels. He's singing as he works. He's drawing several sketches and clearing out his studio."

Suzette listened, without answering.

"Having Hugo to focus on will help him to heal further. Hugo will need him more than ever soon."

Suzette acknowledged the communication in her subconscious. She was aware that Nicole's passing was imminent.

"I do understand what you are saying, Francesca. Thank you for visiting me."

Francesca's fingertips brushed gently across her right cheek and a cool breeze wafted around her.

Coming out of her meditative state, she sat for a while and thought of her precious husband. An opportunity to be 'of service' was being given to him; an opportunity that would fulfil his yearning for parenthood and bring him great joy.

She stood up and walked slowly out of the labyrinth and back to the summer house.

Picking up her pen, she started to write. The words flowed easily, caressing the white sheets with her artistic, delicate strokes.

Stopping for a moment, she poured some water into a glass and sipped it.

The oscillating triangles whispered to her as they moved to and fro; reassuring her that her equilibrium had been restored.

She ate a banana and several grapes as she continued to write; her story unfolding with each newly-filled page.

Glancing at her watch, she realised that she'd been writing for five hours. Where had the time gone?

Gathering up her writing tools, she left the clearing and strolled back towards the house; plucking some peppermint leaves from the herb patch on her way.

She unlocked the door. Serge was still in his studio. Not wanting to disturb him, she filled the kettle with filtered water and dropped several peppermint leaves into a white mug.

Pouring the boiling water onto the leaves, she left it to infuse whilst pondering on her existence. She was grateful for her life.

Sitting down, she reflected on the events of the last seven days. Significant change had taken place and three people were now able to continue on their journey with a renewed sense of purpose.

She'd done what she'd set out to do. She had facilitated the change by providing them with the necessary tools.

Now it was up to them to live the changes and move forward with their lives.

There'd been times during the course when the unwelcome, undulating waves of uncertainty had loomed heavily within the clearing.

Resisting the natural flow of life had caused them emotional unrest. When they'd all willingly released their pain, they'd experienced a new awakening; one which had gifted them with a much clearer understanding and personal growth.

She was confident that manifestation would take place; sooner rather than later!

CHAPTER TWENTY SIX

Suzette was busy preparing the evening meal when Serge came into the kitchen. He leant over her shoulder and kissed her, before going upstairs to shower.

Eve had gone out for the day with Gabriel and wasn't expected for dinner. It would just be the two of them.

Over dinner, Suzette updated Serge on the several chapters she'd managed to complete.

Serge enthused about his rough sketches and his plans for a new sculpture. He'd also tidied his working space.

Suzette already knew what he'd been doing and let him continue speaking.

"I've several ideas rolling around inside my head. I've cleared space in the atelier for when I'm ready. Do you know something, Suzette? My pain has ceased to exist. I thought that I might be aching after all the manual work I've just done but, surprisingly, my back feels so much better. This morning I could sense a difference in my energies."

Suzette served her home-made tarte citron et citron vert with a vanilla ice cream quenelle.

"This is delicious, ma chérie."

She knew it was delicious. She, also, adored the tartness of the lemon and lime.

After clearing the table, they took their wine glasses and sat together on the large sofa; listening to some classical music before falling asleep in each other's arms.

Awakened by Eve's arrival, they yawned and stretched.

Enthused, she relayed the events of her day in Collioure and how they'd visited the Musée d'Art Moderne Fonds Peské to see Serge's sculptures and they'd also been to Les Templiers restaurant.

They both listened attentively as Eve chattered incessantly about how much she'd enjoyed her day. Suzette had half-expected Gabriel to take Eve to Collioure.

Eve had bought three small paintings from an artist who'd been painting beside the harbour. They were semi-abstract in style; muted blues and yellows, depicting the sea, sky and sand.

Serge immediately recognised the style. It was that of a young, talented artist who'd recently moved from nearby Bages, to reside and work in Collioure.

Francois, at twenty eight years of age, was a bachelor; although there was no shortage of women of any age vying to attract his attention. His shoulder-length, black hair and his closely-cropped, sculptured beard complemented his alluring smile and friendly persona. His enigmatic aura was magnetic.

Francois' passion for his work afforded little time for the company of females; except for when his forceful, unrestrained libido demanded their presence. He'd rented a bijou, fisherman's cottage near the outskirts of the village, to soak up the ambience of the area.

He'd had a few girlfriends, but they weren't compatible with his semi-solitary existence and his strong, work ethic.

Eve's excitement over was infectious. Suzette and Serge were more than happy to sit and listen to what Eve had to say.

"I'll just go and make us some hot chocolate. Keep talking, Eve. I can hear you from the kitchen."

Serge slowly heated the milk and made three steaming mugs of hot chocolate to his own special recipe.

"Gabriel's so lovely, Suzette. Not only is he

very attentive, he's so articulate in his perception of the inhumanities and suffering within the world. I can see why he became a doctor", Eve lauded in admiration.

Suzette knew that her friend was 'falling' for Gabriel. She'd known from the moment they'd both set eyes on each other. The attraction was glaringly obvious.

Serge also knew. He smiled as he handed them both the mugs of piping-hot chocolate. Gabriel had spoken, in depth, with him about his sincere admiration for Eve and her understanding, compassionate nature. He'd also told him that he'd felt an intense attraction towards her and that he thought that there was a possibility that she may be 'the one'.

"So, you like him then?" Suzette joked.

She nodded and with raised eyebrows, she pursed her swollen lips. It was clearly obvious that much kissing had taken place.

" I like him – an awful lot. I'm going to see him again tomorrow. He's taken several days off from his work and he's taking me to Narbonne and Perpignan. I'm so excited. I don't think I'll be able to sleep."

Serge handed her the plate of Suzette's home-made, almond biscuits and Eve took one.

"Oh! I think you'll sleep after you've drank my special concoction."

She picked up the mug and took a sip.

"Serge. This is delicious. What have you

put in it?"

"Ah! Well. It's my own secret recipe", he admitted.

Eve dunked the almond biscuit into the hot chocolate and she somehow knew that Serge's secret ingredient wouldn't make her sleep. She was far too excited.

If sleep *did* manage to overcome her, she felt sure that she'd dream of Gabriel.

CHAPTER TWENTY SEVEN

The following morning, after a restless night, Eve awoke to the smell of cooking and the sounds of conversation downstairs. She'd overslept.

A handsome man was coming to collect her at 9.30. Pulling back the curtains, she saw his car parked in the driveway.

Panicking, she looked at the clock. It was 9.15am. He was early!

The adrenalin kicked in as she rushed into the bathroom; quickly showering and brushing her teeth. There was no time to wash her hair, so she snatched it up and held it tight with a large hair slide.

No time for any make-up either. She just moisturized her face, flicked some mascara on her lashes and smeared a lick of gloss over her lips.

Deciding to wear something loose, she grabbed a bright pink, patterned tunic and some turquoise linen trousers out of the armoire and stepped into a pair of white, leather loafers. A quick spray of Tom Ford and she was ready. She didn't want to keep him waiting.

Trying to remain calm, she walked slowly down the stairs, through the kitchen area and out onto the kitchen terrace.

Gabriel came over to greet her. "Bonjour Eve. You look beautiful this morning." He kissed her on both cheeks and as he guided her towards a chair, the butterflies were gaily waltzing from side to side in her stomach.

"Bonjour Gabriel. I have to confess to you that I overslept. "

"Bonjour Suzette. Bonjour Serge."

Suzette chuckled as Serge replied.

"It must have been that hot chocolate eh?"

"It must have been, Serge", she replied, not wanting to offend him.

The hot chocolate hadn't worked. It was her over-excited thoughts that had kept her awake for several hours during the night.

Gabriel accepted the offer to eat some breakfast with them. He'd been too excited to sleep or even eat before he came, but he managed to consume some bread and cheese.

Eve also drank two cups of black coffee before eating some bread, spread thickly with apricot confiture. She was eager to be alone with Gabriel.

"So, which areas are you exploring today", enquired Suzette.

"I thought we might take a leisurely drive into Narbonne and then onto Perpignan, if we have time", answered Gabriel as he cast an admiring glance in Eve's direction.

Eve nodded, delighted at the pleasurable thoughts of having him to herself; all day!

Suzette had already read her thoughts, her smile broadening into a wide grin. Glancing at Eve, she raised her eyebrows and nodded.

Eve tried hard to contain her laughter. She knew what Suzette was thinking.

After they'd finished eating, Eve went upstairs to collect her bag and brush her teeth again.

Suzette had packed several bottles of water and some fruit and nibbles for the journey.

Serge walked to the car with them.

"Enjoy your day. See you later."

"Have a wonderful time" shouted Suzette as she poured a refill of peppermint infusion into her mug.

"We will", replied Gabriel as he took hold of Eve's hand and helped her into the car.

It took approximately forty-five minutes to

reach Narbonne. After parking alongside the Canal de la Robine, they strolled along the tree-lined promenade with its designer boutiques and home-made confectionery shops. Eve, couldn't resist the lure of the sweets, which were inviting her to come in and taste them.

After trying many samples, she bought several chunks of strawberry and lime nougat, covered with meringue. Her sweet tooth was one of her weaknesses. The handsome man, standing close to her, was another!

They continued walking and stopped to sit outside a small café overlooking the impressive, Narbonne Cathedral with its ornate, stained-glass windows.

The waiter approached and took their order.

"Café laiteux pour moi s'il vous plait", replied Gabriel.

"Café noir pour moi s'il vous plait", responded Eve.

Eating chunks of nougat, they chatted about the ancient cathedral. Gabriel explained about the Via Domitia. He also told her about the large, grey uneven boulders of the ancient, Roman roadway which was exposed just in front of where they were sitting.

Eve pondered on how amazing it was to think that, at one time, the Roman soldiers had patrolled the streets of Narbonne.

After drinking their coffee, they made their

way past the Via Domitia and into the Cathedral of St Just et St Pasteur.

On entering the holy place, Eve looked up and was mesmerized by the Gothic style vault, which was more than forty two metres high. The massive tapestries hanging loosely on the walls and the collection of liturgical objects were a magnificent sight to behold.

Eve stopped to look at the 17th century, ornate Baroque organ before making her way to a side chapel, where she lit a candle and knelt down to say a prayer.

Gabriel knelt at the side of her and offered his thanks for recent events.

Leaving the cathedral, they ambled through a maze of uneven cobbled streets, articulating the splendours of the ancient architecture and the cultural aspects of Narbonne.

"Do you like Narbonne, Eve?"

"I love it. I've always taken an interest in architecture and the décor and structures of buildings. I studied some architecture when I was working on my degree".

"I feel as if I have known you for longer than a week, Eve."

" Me, too."

"The last few days have brought a mixture of pleasure and pain, for all of us. The pain being the act of self-purging and the pleasure being the ridding ourselves of defensive mechanisms which were poisoning us."

His eyes lingered on her as she recollected the recent events. Tremors of desire palpated eagerly underneath her breasts and her lower stomach.

"Just being with you, Eve, was pleasurable for me."

Standing in the midst of passing tourists, he took hold of her hand and kissed it, before pulling her close to him and kissing her fully on her pouting lips.

They'd intended travelling into Perpignan. The afternoon had so passed quickly. There wouldn't be enough time to take in the sights.

They decided to return to the Gabriel's house instead. It would be more private there!

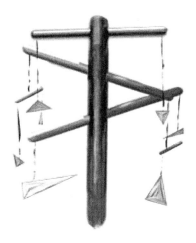

CHAPTER TWENTY EIGHT

Hugo knew her passing was looming; expecting her death was one thing, but the actuality of it was something entirely different.

He'd been beside her bed throughout the long night. Her breathing had slowed down and, at times, he thought that she had left him. Her eyes would open and she would smile at him as if to say "I'm still with you, Hugo".

"I love you Maman", he whispered as he held her hand and kissed her cheeks.

For the past seven hours, he'd repeatedly thanked her for giving him life and believing in him.

He'd tenderly brushed her hair and massaged her hands to warm her. Although he knew from the coldness of her hands that she was slipping away from him, he didn't want to accept that she was dying. How would he survive without her?

Tiredness had eventually taken over his weary body. Surrendering to his fatigue, he closed his eyes momentarily. In his mind's eye, he could see her spirit leaving her body, floating up into the ether. There was another spirit at the side of her, but he didn't know who it was.

Jolted out of his dreamlike state, he could feel his mother's hand gently grip his own. He knew it was her time to leave this earth.

She slowly opened her eyes for the last time, looked deeply into his sad eyes and tilted her head slightly, before closing them again. She had left him.

Sobbing, he clutched tightly onto her still-warm body, hugging it closer to him. As a child, he couldn't bear to be touched by his mother or anyone else; but now all he longed for was his mother to hold him and tell him everything was going to be okay.

A surreal cloak of calmness surrounded him, as if someone was trying to protect him.

He picked up his phone and pressed Serge's number. It rang several times without answer. He pressed the off button and waited. What should he do now?

He sat with her. She looked so serene after

all the pain she'd endured. He knew she couldn't take any more suffering and it was selfish of him to have wanted her to remain with him. He knew that she'd unconditionally forfeited her own life when she was younger, to care for him and for that he was more than grateful. His mother was the only one who really understood him.

He kissed her forehead and her face was still warm.

"Come to me in my dreams and talk to me", he whispered in her ear.

Her voice came through to him, although it was the voice of when she was younger; before Parkinson's had taken hold of her body and mind.

"I will, my son. I promise you. I'm not in any pain now."

He smiled through his tears. He knew that the strong emotional bond which they'd shared, more so over the last ten years, could never be broken.

His phone rang. It was Serge.

"Serge, he cried. She's gone. She's gone."

"I'm coming over now."

Hurriedly, Serge ended the call and shouted to Suzette. She was preparing breakfast with Eve in the kitchen.

"Quickly, Suzette. Nicole has just passed over. We need to go to Hugo, now."

Leaving Eve, they both sprinted down the driveway and climbed over the fence into Nicole's garden, before running along the path and into the open, front door where they found Hugo huddled over Nicole's body.

Serge went over to him and tried to ease him away from Nicole.

"Come Hugo."

Hugo resisted, enfolding her body tightly with his own.

"No, Serge. Just let me hold her for a little longer. I don't want them to take her."

Serge didn't force him. He'd felt the same when his own mother had died. He walked over to Suzette and hugged her.

"Go to him, Suzette, he whispered. He needs you."

Suzette approached Hugo and released his grip from Nicole. She held him close to her and she could feel the pain emanating from his limp body. She took him into the kitchen where Serge had infused some herbs and handed him the filled cup. Respecting his need for silence, she just sat next to him with her arm around him. She couldn't find the words to comfort him and so she waited until he spoke, or rather shouted!

"Why did it have to happen? Why did *she* have to die now and leave me? I don't understand what life is all about", he screamed. "I loved her. I still love her."

Serge had been outside ringing the doctor and rushed back in when he heard Hugo's raised voice.

He went over to Hugo and sat at the other

side of him. He understood his anger and the way his autism presented itself when he was stressed.

"She knew that you loved her and she loved you too, Hugo. She could see the way you cared for her throughout her illness. She knew that you were devoted to her."

The doctor let himself in. He nodded towards Suzette and Serge and went over to Nicole. After examining Nicole's body, he issued a *certifat de deces* and told Serge that Nicole's death must be registered within twenty-four hours at the Mairie.

Serge respectfully nodded. He was already aware of procedures; he had buried his wife, his own mother and his father in recent years. He knew how to notify all the appropriate authorities and would take care of all the details.

Nicole had already completed the necessary paperwork regarding her last will and testament, when she'd discovered that she was in the final stages of her life. She'd divorced her husband two years after he'd left them. The house had been part of the hefty divorce settlement; as was the continuing yearly allowance until Hugo was thirty. The house already belonged to Hugo. The bank account was in joint names. Everything was bequeathed to Hugo.

After the doctor had left, Hugo sat alone with his mother for a short while before Suzette took him back to their home. The doctor had left some medication for Hugo; aware that he'd not been sleeping and would need to get some rest.

The funeral directors came and removed Nicole's body. As Serge turned the key in the door, an unexpected chilling breeze wafted past him; shivering as the winds of change hovered around him.

CHAPTER TWENTY NINE

They'd stayed up until the early hours of the morning, talking about Nicole.

Periods of silence occasionally dominated the conversation with unexpected, gut-wrenching outbursts of anger from Hugo.

"Why did if have to happen, Serge? Why? Why?"

Serge could relate to his outbursts. He'd felt the same way when Francesca and his parents had died. He also knew that no one could ever feel or know the true depth of another's grief. Sorrow is individual and diverse. He wouldn't dare patronise Hugo by saying that he understood. It would be insensitive of him to do so.

Moving closer to Hugo on the sofa, he put his arm around him.

"What am I going to do without her, Serge?"

"You can stay here with us for as long as you feel you want to. We made a promise that we would take care of you and help with the house and other arrangements."

Suzette closely observed the way Serge gently comforted him. She'd noticed a bond developing between them both, especially since Nicole first declared the severity of her illness.

"Serge. This searing pain burns inside my head and scorches my chest. It won't go away. I feel empty. I can't believe that she's gone."

Suzette had subtly dropped the sleep-inducing medication into Hugo's drink. He was exhausted; having had little sleep whilst caring for his mother. It was his choice to stay awake. He'd wanted to spend as much time alone with her as he could. Time had been precious and he'd had no control over it. The time he'd had with her was not long enough!

Suzette could see that the medication was beginning to take effect. He was finding it difficult to keep his eyes open.

"Shall we try and get some sleep? You must be exhausted, Hugo."

The room in which he would sleep had

previously been prepared, in anticipation of the unwanted event. It was at the rear of the house, overlooking farmland and orchards.

Reluctantly, Hugo allowed Serge to direct him to his room. He didn't want to sleep. He wanted his mother.

Whilst Suzette's tiredness had overcome her almost immediately, Serge lay awake, ruminating about how Hugo would cope. Over the past six months, a profound change had occurred within him. Nicole's deterioration had triggered a sense of responsibility. He was now acquainted with the challenges that life brings and the amount of strength that is required to overcome them.

Serge got up and crept along the corridor to where Hugo was sleeping. He was crouched, in the feotal position, hugging himself.

He pulled the sheet over him. Thankfully, exhaustion had Hugo in its grip and now he could get some rest. It was heart-rendering to see him in this state.

Tomorrow, they were expected to travel north for the unveiling ceremony of his sculpture. He'd telephone the Chief Executive and explain his predicament.

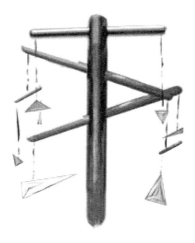

CHAPTER THIRTY

The days which followed Nicole's passing were an excruciatingly painful blur for him. Things didn't seem real and he'd had trouble functioning. On unexpected occasions, an intense grief would surge up from within his gut and grip his throat tightly; threatening to strangle him until he could no longer breathe.

Nevertheless, he insisted on going with Serge to gather the paperwork and make the necessary arrangements for his mother's funeral.

Serge had returned to the house with Hugo to collect some clean clothes and toiletries. Hugo half-expected his mother to still be there; lying in her bed.

Whilst Serge and Hugo were out, Suzette had been across to Nicole's house to tidy around. Nicole's spirit was still hovering. She could sense her; as could Hugo when he'd had been there earlier!

Over the following days, the three of them visited the clearing; sometimes just sitting together inside the summer house and, at other times, meditating in the labyrinth.

"I can feel her with me, Suzette. She is here with us now." Hugo's intuitive senses had been heightened in his time of sorrow.

"Yes, Hugo. Your mother's spirit is here. I can feel her presence too."

The daily visits had a calming effect on him. His appetite had returned and he was eating more than he'd done in the recent months.

After eating his evening meal, he'd excuse himself and go to his room. He wanted to be alone with his grief and prepare the eulogy. The script had been written several times. When he thought he'd completed it, he would remember other things that he wanted to include.

Writing down his thoughts was therapeutic for him. Recalling specific events throughout his life and putting pen to paper was part of a clearing process.

He'd been journalling his thoughts and feelings for several months. Entries included the way he felt about his father abandoning them both, his autism and his fear of the unknown. His writing had been precise; remembering every minute detail, writing about his emotions and how he'd tried to rationalise them. He'd even sketched some images of seeds, which he had aptly labelled 'seeds of doubt being sown' and a vague image of his father.

The eulogy was completed. In two days' time he would say his farewell to his precious mother.

After dinner one evening, Hugo asked Suzette and Serge if they'd listen to what he'd wrote. He wanted to practice the eulogy in front of them, to see if it was appropriate.

Rising from his chair, he unfolded his speech and started to read Nicole's eulogy. His calm voice was pitch-perfect and his articulation painted a faultless picture of Nicole.

The admiration that Serge felt for Hugo was immense. The young man had displayed a strength of character which was way beyond his years; a strength which he'd acquired from Nicole!

Suzette's mothering instincts kicked in. She walked over to him and hugged him; wanting to alleviate his pain and suffering. She knew that he'd have to go through the pain and suffering himself! When she'd first met Hugo he didn't like being tactile, but he had, over time, become more emotionally aware.

She too, would miss Nicole. She had

enjoyed exchanging views and theories with her. Suzette had learnt more about how Hugo's autism had presented itself. It was as if Nicole wanted her to know all about him, so that she'd understand and accept the reasons behind his 'sometimes bizarre' and vulnerable behaviour.

Suzette recognised that understanding was key. Embracing difference was key. Labelling was unfair; as was being judged for being different. She knew also that intelligence comes in many forms. She'd witnessed it on numerous occasions.

The words in Hugo's eulogy rang in her ears. His well-chosen words were so relevant. They captured the essence of Nicole's personality and her purpose for living; that purpose being to rear and care for her only son!

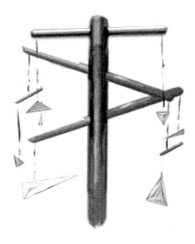

CHAPTER THIRTY ONE

The funeral was a private affair. Nicole had wanted it that way. Serge had dealt with the necessary arrangements; obtaining the Le Certificat medical de Deces and the L'acte de déces. Only six people were in attendance and the person who performed the ceremony.

Hugo, Serge, Gabriel and the family doctor carried Nicole's body into the crematorium from the hearse, which had parked outside the entrance. Nicole didn't want a burial.

The undertakers waited outside after they

had supervised the carrying of the coffin.

A delicate arrangement of assorted flowers, which Hugo had picked from Nicole's garden, was placed on top of the coffin.

In compliance with the law, the cremation had to be carried out within seven days and, exactly one week after Nicole's passing, her body was now waiting to be cremated.

In stark contrast to his previous dishevelled appearance, Hugo was now clean-shaven and his hair had been cut short. Dressed in a black suit, he stood tall and upright in front of his mother's coffin; clutching his carefully written eulogy. She would have been proud of him.

As he spoke of his mother's love of life and the way she'd loved him and taken care of him, he could hear the women crying. There'd be time for shedding his own tears later, in private.

Her fragrant perfume permeated his nostrils and he heard her softly-spoken voice.

"Hugo, know that I love you. I have loved you from the very moment I conceived you and I will still love you whilst I am in spirit. When you feel a gentle breeze, I will be beside you. I will come to you in your dreams. I will guide you through your life. You'll never be alone. I'll always be with you. Celebrate my life today and live your life to the full. Sadness surrounds you now, but you'll be happy one day, my precious son."

Hugo ended the eulogy by bidding his mother farewell. He bent down and kissed her coffin.

"Au revoir maman."

The music started to play and, as the conveyor started moving, the drapes closed around Nicole's coffin and she was taken away.

Devastated as he was, Hugo continued to remain strong and, when the music had stopped playing, he stepped down from the podium and joined the others, before walking outside into the brilliant sunshine.

Authorisation had been granted for Nicole's ashes to be dispersed on her own land. He would wait for the telephone call to collect her ashes the following day. Hugo would keep her close to him, before deciding on a suitable location within the garden to lay her to rest.

They all returned to Villa d'Couture Atelier. Suzette had prepared lunch for them and before they ate, they lifted their champagne filled flutes in celebration of Nicole's life.

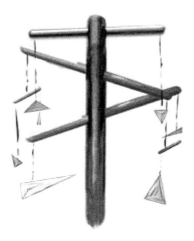

CHAPTER THIRTY TWO

At 9.30 am, Eve and Gabriel boarded the plane at Tolouse Blagnac Airport for the early morning flight to Leonardo da Vinci, Flamicino Airport; the busiest airport in Italy.

The flight would only be a short one, lasting one hour and forty five minutes.

Impulsively, they'd spent a whole afternoon a few days earlier, planning their journey to the seductive and charming Amalfi coast.

In the 1920's and 1930's it had been a popular holiday haunt for the upper class and the privileged aristocracy. Nowadays, all statuses chose to holiday there.

Eve had read a short story called 'Positano' by John Steinbeck, which he'd wrote in 1953 and she'd also watched 'Under the Tuscan Sun' on video, numerous times. Positano, a village on the Amalfi coast, had also featured in that film. She was so looking forward to visiting some of the places along the vertiginous coastlines.

After landing, they collected their luggage and their hire care before driving along many hairpin turns and narrow roads through Frosinone and Cassini; finally stopping in Caserto to rest, drink coffee and eat.

"I'm really looking forward to visiting Capri and Herculaneum and Pompeii and Vesuvius; and not forgetting Sorrento and Positano", Eve rambled on excitedly.

Gabriel clung onto every solitary word she spoke, as he reached over the table to take hold of her hand.

"Me, too. I love exploring. This is exactly what I want to do in my retirement. We've planned the itinerary and now we're going to have an amazing time."

They finished their coffee and returned to the car.

After several hour's driving through the rugged shorelines and pastel coloured, fishing villages, passing through Sorrento and above Positano, they finally reached Amalfi in the late afternoon.

The journey, although interesting, had been quite daunting, with many unpredictable Italians speeding past and overtaking them on the hairpin bends.

They checked into their hotel and were taken up to their room, which was situated on the third floor overlooking the Piazza del Duomo. It had a small balcony with a magnificent view of the ocean.

After unpacking their luggage, they sat on the balcony drinking coffee and eating several almond biscotti and tiny macarons filled with lemon-verbena ganache; courtesy of the hotel.

Relaxing, they watched the holidaymakers and the locals as they strolled by, eating their gelatos and chatting incessantly.

"Let's go exploring. I'm eager to taste some of those gelatos. I've promised myself that I'm going to try a different flavour every day", Eva declared as she collected the cups and went inside.

Collecting their hats and sunglasses, Gabriel locked the door and they made their way onto the Piazza.

Their first port of call was *Cioccolato* e *Gelato Andrea Pansa.* The intoxicating smell of the tempting chocolates, displayed artistically in cool glass cabinets, teased Eve as she walked through the open doorway.

Gazing longingly at the array of dark, milk and white chocolates, skillfully decorated with ginger and almonds, Eve's saliva glands were instantly triggered.

A young, slim lady with raven-black hair, coiled into a perfectly coiffured top-knot welcomed them.

Confidently balancing an oblong, silver tray, carefully arranged with rows of mouth-watering chocolates, she smiled and invited them both to sample them.

Eve took one and placed it into her mouth. The rich, creamy texture of the milk chocolate melted on her tongue before a burst of softened, salted caramel exploded and coated the roof of her mouth.

"Ah! Gabriel. This is delicious. Try one."

The assistant handed him the tray and he took one. His saliva glands were already in overdrive as he inhaled the intoxicating, heady aroma of the chocolate and, as the lusciously-liquified filling dissolved within his mouth, his tongue's receptors tingled and he closed his eyes for a few seconds, savouring the delightful aftertaste.

"Deliziosi", he declared.

As the assistant held out the tray once more, it was clearly obvious that she was passionate about chocolate and that she'd also been trained to be customer focused.

Eve chose a small, dark chocolate which was infused with ginger. It was only at the last moment that the warm, spicy liquid leaked onto her tongue and she coughed slightly.

Gabriel refused another chocolate. He would have some later.

After buying two boxes of assorted chocolates, they left the chocolatiers and strolled, arm in arm, towards the cathedral which took pride of place in the Piazza del Duomo.

Eve was a little breathless as she climbed the wide, steep steps up to massive, bronze doors of the Romanesque Baroque cathedral; sixty two steps in total.

They both stared in awe at the magnificence which stood before them. Above the glorious altar was a painting of The Martyrdom of St Andrew, whose relics were kept in a tomb in the crypt.

Absorbing the peaceful ambience they moved along two aisles which were divided by twenty marble columns. Several large paintings and a bronze statue of St Andrew adorned the spacious basilica. An elderly guide, expressively gestured towards each piece of art and his evenly-paced, carefully-pronounced tones described how relics of St Andrew had been brought from Constantinople in 1206.

After cautiously tackling their way down the sixty two steps, they mingled with holidaymakers and locals until they reached their hotel room.

Eve stepped out of her glitzy sandals and went to shower. She desperately needed to cool down. The afternoon heat had drained her.

As she emerged from the shower, draped in

a white, cotton dressing gown, Gabriel was lying on the bed, naked. He opened his eyes and gazed longingly at her as she approached him.

His urge to caress her sun-kissed body was uncontrollable and, as he stretched over towards her, he loosened the cord of her dressing gown. It fell to the floor and he pulled her onto the bed.

She didn't resist as he delicately circled her lips with his own. The manly fragrance of his skin and his day's growth of beard prickled her and rapid ripples of excitement pirouetted around her sacral region.

Exploring her shapely curves, he kissed and delicately stroked the outline of her body. As she silently surrendered to the sensual touch of his lips and finger tips, she lay back and soaked in his selfless attention to her desires, anticipating the imminent act of passion.

Running her long fingers through his hair, she brought his face towards hers, kissing him with an extreme intenseness that both jolted him and roused him. He responded with an equal intensity and, as their hormone levels intensified their eager connection, she changed her tactics and gently used her fingertips to examine his muscled torso and his firm legs.

Gabriel's back arched as he awaited her next touch, with its promise of electrifying tremors.

Unable to wait any longer, they encouraged the forceful energy to flow through their entwined bodies by moving rhythmically and frenetically, until their needs were fulfilled.

Curling his body around hers, he held onto her tightly. He knew that he wanted to be with her. His prior melancholy was dissipating and he was looking forward to a future with her; if she wanted him!

Interrupting the silence, she spoke.

"I've just remembered something from this afternoon, Gabriel."

"What have you remembered, Eve?

Her eyes glistened as she laughed.

"I didn't have a gelato earlier. I was going to have a dark chocolate straciatella."

He grinned at her and raised his eyebrows. Her dry sense of humour was only one of the many things that he loved about her.

"Well Eve, I wouldn't want you to miss out on having your daily quota. We'll call for one later."

CHAPTER THIRTY THREE

Over the following days they visited several art galleries, absorbed the many spectacular views of nature, watched a romantic wedding in Ravello, took a boat over to the romantic island of Capri and sunbathed on the beaches in Positano and Sorrento.

They ate first-class, mouthwatering food and different flavours of gelato, drank fine wines and limoncello, laughed and loved; passionately and frequently!

Gabriel was falling for Eve. He knew that he loved her when she'd openly expressed her views on the course. She'd awakened something in his heart. He didn't want the holiday to end.

Eve, too, was experiencing flutters. Could this be the man she'd been waiting for? Could he be the one that would heal her heart?

After the plane had landed at Tolouse Blagnac Airport, they collected their luggage and walked to the car park.

On the way home they travelled in silence; neither one of them wanting to acknowledge that it was time for them to return to reality. Excitedly, they'd spoken about spending more time together and had discussed exploring other countries.

Eve didn't want to continue with her design consultancy. She wanted to be with Gabriel.

Gabriel was never more certain of his decision to retire. There was a sense of oneness when he was with her.

"I know you're leaving tomorrow, Eve. When will you return?"

"I have several large contracts that are nearing completion. Once they've been finalised, I will be free to return."

He smiled at the thought of her returning.

"Would it be rude of me to ask whether you will take on any more contracts, Eve?"

Looking straight into his eyes, she replied with her own question.

"Why do you ask, Gabriel?"

"I ask because I'd like you to live with me, here in France. We could use my home as a base and then travel the world and enjoy new experiences, together. Now that I've found you, I don't want to lose you."

She tried to catch her breath. Her heart was dancing a tango.

"I was waiting to see if you felt the same way as I did, before I accepted new contracts. I would love to live with you here. In the short time that I have known you, I've fallen in love with you."

Taking her in his arms, he held her tightly. Her words echoed his own as he whispered in her ear.

"Ma chérie. I love you too. You're the one I've been waiting for."

She smiled; tears trickling down her cheek.

"Why do you cry?"

"They are only tears of happiness, Gabriel. Although, I am a little sad, knowing that I'll be leaving you tomorrow."

They both knew that the next few months would be filled with many responsibilities and closures; all of which would allow them to finally be together.

CHAPTER THIRTY FOUR

Stephanie Stark, an established photographer, was well-known for her diverse, thought-provoking and controversial images.

She'd used her single name when originally building her personal brand and had retained it after her marriage, purely for professional and promotional purposes.

In a profession which is usually dominated by men, Stephanie's contemporary and challenging technique had won her several prestigious awards. Her ability to ingeniously capture unimaginable images of people, architecture and meaningful environmental and social issues, had gained her recognition, both nationally and internationally. Her innovative potential had not, in any way, been restricted by her femininity.

Inherited from her resilient mother, her intuitive quirkiness had evolved and flourished since her childhood days when, camera in hand, she'd taken copious amounts of photographs of family members, nature and obscure objects.

Sitting on a hard, metal bench in the arrivals area of John Lennon Airport in Liverpool, she waited excitedly for her mother to arrive on the early afternoon flight from Carcassonne.

It had been a while since her mother's last visit. She facetimed regularly to keep her updated and to ensure that her children had some contact with their grandmama.

Over the last fifteen years, Stephanie had developed a strong bond with her mother. It had not always been so. As a child and a teenager, she knew that her stubborn streak and her periodic, negative moods were testing for her mother. Her mother had understood her. She'd encouraged her daughter's spirit; accepting that it was part of who Stephanie was and it being her baptism into adult life.

Her career and motherhood had changed her. Having her own children had made her realise how much her mother had sacrificed when she was bringing up two children, alone.

Although they clashed at times with their

differing views, she had a profound admiration for her mother. Her mother had always motivated both her and her elder brother to have a 'voice'. Stephanie was confident with expressing her own opinions; especially about many humane issues which she felt strongly about.

Influenced by her mother's compassionate nature, love of art and creative talent, Stephanie had ventured into the highly-competitive world of photography after graduating from John Moore's University with a BA Honours Degree in Fine Art.

She smiled to herself as her mother's words of wisdom echoed loudly within the corridors of her sub-conscious. "Do your best and learn as much as you can, Stephanie."

Standing up, she walked over to the electronic information board. Her mother's flight had just landed, but it would be another twenty minutes or so before she walked through the double doors with her suitcase trailing behind her.

Stephanie's heart skipped a beat, her emotions misting her vision as her mother frantically waved her hand to alert her arrival.

Rushing over to Stephanie, Suzette hugged her daughter tightly.

Incessantly chattering, the pair walked over to the car park and continued with their animated conversation whilst driving to Stephanie's house in the Mossley Hill area of Liverpool.

Charlie, a chocolate-brown Labrador, had his paws on the window sill as they pulled into the drive.

As Suzette opened the front door, he jumped up at them and excitedly ran around their feet until they made a fuss of him.

Before entering the living area, Stephanie and Suzette removed their shoes in the genken hall area and stepped into some slippers.

The house was peaceful. The children were at school. Yoshio, Stephanie's husband, was out visiting a new client in the city.

She had met Yoshio Takada when she was on an important photography assignment in Japan. He was the architect who had designed all of the buildings which she had been commissioned to photograph, for a well-known architectural journal.

There was an instant attraction. Their artistic commonalities, sense of humour and love of all types of art had brought them together; or had they been the architects of their own fate?

After a two-year, long-distance relationship, Stephanie had persuaded the ambitious Yoshio to broaden his horizons and he'd willingly agreed to come over to England to live with her. They married soon after and had two children within a period of two years. Toshika, their son, was now ten years old and Toshira, their daughter, was nine.

England had benefitted greatly from the innovative, minimalist architect. Yoshio had been instrumental in the conceptual design and the personal overseeing of the construction of new apartments on the waterfront in Liverpool. He'd also designed other developments on the outskirts of Manchester and in the city centre.

Yoshio still travelled the world asserting his skills. A devoted father and husband, he'd made a pact with himself that he wouldn't be away from home for periods lasting more than two weeks at one given time. He'd honoured his word.

When the couple were newly-wed, they lived in Stephanie's semi-detached house. By chance, they managed to acquire a substantial plot of land. Jointly, they had designed a unique, geometric-shaped dwelling to suit their uncluttered lifestyle.

Open-plan in design, with large and small windows punctured irregularly into a white concrete block, some of their neighbours had likened their home to a cold, white chunk of stone and glass; characterless and non-descript. Those same neighbours had objected strongly to their plans. Fortunately, a young up-and-coming town planner with an unconventional, creative vision, welcomed the opportunity to make his mark. He gave permission for the functional, minimalistic piece of art to be constructed.

As Suzette walked into the bright living space, she was overcome as always, with the ambience. She loved this house. She'd been excited when it was being built; overseeing every single stage of its construction. Thirty years earlier, she'd jointly partaken in the design and construction of a modern dwelling; Scandinavian in design and unlike any other house in the area where she lived.

She gazed, admiringly, at the enormous, first-floor cube-shaped studio which appeared to float effortlessly over the external courtyard. This space was jointly inhabited by Stephanie and Yoshio.

Artwork in the form of blurred images of her grandchildren were beamed onto the stark, white walls from an ingeniously-concealed projector. Miniscule splashes of primary colours in the form of obscure objects gave warmth to the main living area.

Over lunch comprising of sushi and fruit salad, they discussed Stephanie's forthcoming exhibition, which was to be held at the Tate Gallery on the Albert Dock in Liverpool. A whole floor had been allocated for her rare collection of contemporary images, depicting the honest and sensitive human emotions of all gender.

Rejecting conventional expectations, her sole intention was to entice the viewer to linger and subconsciously challenge the motives that lie behind her compelling and complex images.

"The opening of my latest exhibition is at 1.00pm on Saturday. It'll be a private viewing until 3.00pm and then it will be open for public viewing. The theme is entitled 'Emotional Equality' and my intention is to provoke and evoke!"

"Oh! I'm certain your work will provoke and evoke. It always does. The high ceilings in the

Tate will allow excellent exposure for the larger exhibits. Having the whole floor will easily accommodate the viewers comfortably. I can't wait to see them."

"Yoshio is bringing some of his clients. They're interested in buying pieces of my work for their show homes. There should be about thirty of us in total, so it shouldn't be too crowded. The children are excited. I recently exhibited a small collection in the gallery at Bluecoat Chambers, depicting the innocence of children. It got some great reviews."

"I read the reviews online, Stephanie. They were very impressive."

As Stephanie cleared the plates from the table, Charlie hovered impatiently. It was time for his walk.

"Shall we take Charlie for a stroll before we collect the children from school, Mum?"

"Yes. That would be good. I need to stretch my legs after that plane journey."

CHAPTER THIRTY FIVE

Saturday morning arrived. Yoshio was busy in the kitchen space, cooking breakfast. Stephanie was answering endless emails and Suzette was with her grandchildren playing a game on the Xbox.

"Grandmama, you need to be quick. Toshira will catch you", advised Toshika.

"Toshika, my brain isn't as young as yours, you know. What should I have done?"

"You should have been concentrating on the game, Grandmama. Toshira will win now."

Yoshio and Stephanie looked at each other and could hardly contain their laughter. Their children were very competitive and advanced in their use of all technology.

"Ok, Toshika. I will try harder next time", she promised.

"Come on over, everyone. Breakfast is ready", Yoshio beckoned.

On weekends and some nights in the week, they ate Japanese style. Yoshio was adamant that his children would know about their heritage and he wanted them to respect Japanese customs.

Both children were bilingual. Yoshio spoke to them in his mother tongue on a daily basis. It was the only way for them to learn the language. They received home tuition from a native Japanese tutor, who visited once a week. Stephanie also joined in the lessons.

"Toshira, Toshika. *Ima sugu chōshoku o tabete*", their father prompted again, asking them to come and eat their breakfast.

"Sumimasen, Papa. Watashitachi wa ima sugu ni kite iru", Toshika replied. The children obeyed his instruction and they moved over to the table.

The five of them feasted on grilled fish, rice, nori, miso soup and Japanese pickles. The healthy breakfast would nourish them until just after the exhibition, when refreshments would be served.

Yoshio poured boiling water onto the green tea leaves. A pot containing peppermint leaves was already infusing for Suzette.

Suzette was very proud of the way her

daughter and Yoshio were rearing their children. She cherished the moment, as she watched her grandson niftily fill a sheet of dried seaweed with some fish and sticky rice. He dipped it into some soy sauce before advising her again.

"Grandmama, you should really practice the game when you go home. Then, you will be able to win next time."

She nodded her head and tried not to laugh at what he had said. In a way, he was right. Practice makes perfect, but she wasn't interested in playing any games on the Xbox."

"I will try, Toshika."

After a varied conversation about school life, work, current affairs and Suzette's life in France, each of them helped to clear the table and fill the dishwasher before getting ready for the exhibition.

As they had all assembled in the hall, Yoshio smiled at Stephanie and nodded his head slowly.

She raised her eyebrows and shrugged her shoulders; silently questioning his gestures.

"Your mother has satori, Stephanie. She has a silent understanding. There is a calmness and an aura all around her", he whispered.

The children heard him and Toshika spoke.

"Papa. What is satori?"

"Satori is the Japanese word for meaningful insight, Toshika. It is a state of mind."

Toshika and Toshira looked puzzled, whilst Suzette smiled, knowingly. She'd never heard of satori before, but she knew exactly what Yoshio was referring to.

Toshiro interrupted.

"What is a state of mind, Papa? I don't know what you mean."

Yoshio pointed to a framed symbol which was hung on the wall nearest to the front door. It was simple in design and its bold, black brushstrokes stood proud against the white background.

"Have you never wondered what this symbol is? Satori is about having a deeper, spiritual experience. My dearest children, I will explain the meaning in detail to you at another time. In the way we already live our lives, we are all practising satori."

Stephanie recalled the conversations with her husband about Zen, mental calmness and living in the present moment.

Suzette smiled.

Yoshio turned to his children and placed his arms around their shoulders.

"It is my greatest wish that you both possess satori. I want you to know who you are and why you are here on this earth. However, you will only understand satori when you have experienced many, earthly challenges as you follow your own paths."

Stephanie looked at her watch. As much as she would have liked him to continue with the conversation, time would not allow it.

They left at 11.30 prompt. Stephanie wanted to give herself time to check, once more, that everything was as it should be. Over-scrupulous about everything associated with her work, she had supervised the siting and the hanging of each exhibit. She had her reputation to uphold and exactness was imperative if she were to engage her audience and convince them of the importance of her theme.

Already, she'd received several requests from people wanting to buy her work, after reading an article on her website. On her last update she had showcased several of the images which would be included in the exhibition , scheduled to last for two weeks. Wanting to influence others, she had also submitted a whole collection of her work to Unsplash; an impactful website which shares copyright free photography, allowing others to use it freely.

Stephanie would exhibit her work in two more locations before deciding on which images she would sell. The interested buyers would have to wait a little longer!

Together with her children and her husband, Stephanie watched as the barriers surrounding the exhibition were deftly removed. They would be reinstalled once all the guests had arrived for the private viewing.

Welcoming her guests, she introduced them to her family, before directing them towards the different viewing areas.

Suzette watched from a distance as the visitors milled around the exhibits. She wanted to observe the viewers' reactions and eavesdrop into their conversations, so that she could feedback to her daughter later on.

"So, what made you want to use 'Emotional Equality' as your theme then?" The quirky, young journalist held his mobile phone in close proximity to Suzette, to record the interview before writing his review. Later, it would be adapted for use in several journals and publications.

"I wanted to highlight the shift that is currently being witnessed in areas of gender equality. My aim is to portray the strengths and weaknesses of all gender and the diverse human emotions they experience in their lives. It's not intended to be a political statement. It's more about provoking self-awareness in each and every one of us; how we should respect the feelings and sensitivities of every human being, irrespective of gender."

"Interestingly, you have shot some images that depict mental health issues, disability, childbirth, war and achievement; all disparate and yet all comparable in your effort to promote emotional equality."

Stephanie guided the journalist towards a photograph depicting raw emotion, to reinforce her chosen theme.

"Yes. These images are intended to evoke emotions. I want the viewer to really feel every expression and gesture. In my opinion, the release of all emotions is healthy; although I think that some heterosexual, alpha-males may disagree with my views on shedding tears."

Without speaking, the journalist nodded in agreement.

"This particular shot shows the abject pain and anguish of a man sobbing over the dying body of his disabled, best friend. It had a profound effect on me after I had taken it. I did get permission from both of the men to take it. I took many of more of them showing extreme happiness. Take a look at this one."

She stopped for a moment, remembering the first moment she'd met the men and recalled the fond friendship she'd nurtured with them. They'd attended many of her exhibitions and she liked their openness and their honest critique.

"Hegemonic masculinity and cultural dynamics have determined that it was not acceptable for a man to cry in public. A 'stiff upper lip' was required at all times. This tradition is outdated. Recent statistics have revealed that a sizeable proportion of the younger generation have rejected the tradition, embracing the belief that it is acceptable for a man to show his feelings and cry. It is acceptable for a man to be in touch with his feminine side, without being discriminated against. Human sentiments are complex and feelings should be acknowledged, without fear of judgement. We are not robots."

The journalist switched off his phone. He was crying. The image had resurrected the recent passing of his own partner, who had succumbed to cancer. After initial diagnosis, he'd desperately clung onto his life for six months.

"I can resonate with both of those images. I lost my beloved partner four months ago. The cruel clutches of cancer claimed his life. It's difficult for me to carry on without him. I'm so grateful that I met him and for the time I had with him. He was a gentle soul."

Stephanie hugged him. Aware that others were watching, she escorted him away from the viewing area and into a side room. Handing him some tissues, she listened to him. It was important to listen to him pour out his grief and share his longing for the man he had loved – and lost.

Suzette, who had been talking to her grandchildren, had noticed the incident. She'd suggested that boxes of tissues be strategically placed around the viewing space in anticipation of unexpected, emotional outpourings. Many unprepared viewers made good use of them.

The ambience within the viewing space was juxtaposed with an equal mixture of elation and sadness. The intentional theme, which depicted the complexity of human behaviour, had produced the reactions that Stephanie wanted; the releasing of all emotions.

Suzette could see much of her own inspiration in her daughter's approach to the human psyche. Her influence had been instantly recognizable in the way Stephanie cared about people and the way in which she promoted the need for self-awareness in all gender.

Whilst the guests adjourned to an adjoining room for light refreshments, Yoshio instructed the guides and security team to allow the eagerly-awaiting public viewers into the exhibition.

Once the many questions had been answered and refreshments had been consumed, Stephanie thanked everyone for attending and gathered her family together, before returning home.

She'd achieved what she'd set out to do!

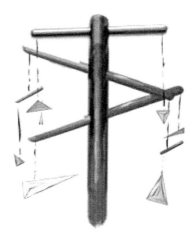

CHAPTER THIRTY SIX

Hugo awoke early. He sensed her presence. She was with him when he went to sleep, in his dreams and always when he woke up. There was a strong smell of lavender, like the hand and body lotion that he'd massaged her with when she was ailing. In his latest dream, his cherished mother was in her garden, tending to her flowers. She looked so beautiful, younger and happy.

Since she'd passed over, he'd seen her several times and he always knew when she was near him.

Sometimes, he would see her at the end of

his bed, in the floral dress that she loved to wear. At first, he would open and close his eyes, in disbelief, but she would remain there for a while, watching over him.

He heard her voice; loud and clear.

"Never forget, Hugo, that I'll always be with you and never forget that I love you."

"Oh! Maman. Thank you for coming to me."

He could hear Serge preparing breakfast. He hurled back the cotton sheet, threw on a tee shirt and stepped into his shorts.

"Bonjour, Serge", he greeted him as he walked into the kitchen.

"Bonjour Hugo. Did you sleep well?"

"I did, thank you."

Serge smiled.

"Can I help you with preparing the breakfast, Serge?"

"It's nearly finished, Hugo. Could you set the table and fill the jug with orange juice?"

Hugo nodded and went outside to the kitchen terrace to prepare the table.

Over breakfast they chatted about gardening and the harvesting of the fruits and vegetables in both of their gardens.

Before going to the labyrinth to meditate, they had decided go over the Hugo's house to gather some crops from Nicole's vegetable patch.

Hugo surprised Serge with his unforeseen question.

"Will you adopt me, Serge? I want to call you père. You have been more of a father to me than the man whose name I bear. He has never been a father to me. Even when I was a child, he would look at me with utter disdain, as if I wasn't worthy enough to be his child. You respect my views. You listen to me. I don't feel insignificant when I am with you and Suzette."

Serge's eyes glistened, almost choking on his reply.

"Oh. Hugo. I don't know if it's possible for me to adopt you. You are nineteen."

They both laughed, but Hugo was serious.

"I want to be your son, Serge. I want to take your name. I want to change my name to Hugo Couture."

Hugo's voice quivered as he continued.

"He wasn't there to teach me things when I was growing up. I had no one to teach me 'men' things; even how to shave. Maman showed me, but I missed having a man to guide me."

He wiped a stray tear.

"If I ever have a child, Serge, I'll teach it lots of things and I'll spend time with it. I'll give the child everything that I didn't get from my own père. I would be a good père, Serge."

Serge would love Hugo to be known as his son. It was all he'd ever wanted when he was married to Francesca; to have a son and teach him things and play games with him, like his father had done with him.

"If you want to, Hugo, you can call me Père. It will be an honour for you to call me by that name."

Serge and Hugo had formed an even closer bond whilst Suzette had been in England. It was as if she'd known that their time together would be healing for them both.

Together, they cleared the breakfast table and strolled over to collect some green beans, onions and potatoes from Nicole's garden.

Although tinged with sadness, the house and garden had a welcoming feel. Surprisingly, Hugo was feeling stronger as he opened the back door of his house. His mother's smell still lingered and he smiled, remembering her mannerisms.

Whilst Serge was busy collecting vegetables, Hugo took several items of clothing from his armoire and placed them into a holdall.

After securing the door, they went back to Villa d'Couture Atelier. Depositing the freshly-picked vegetables on the kitchen terrace, they made their way over to the clearing.

The oscillating triangles swayed gently as they stepped onto the shimmering, mosaic path which led them to the centre of the labyrinth.

The water soothed them as it cascaded down the triangular sculpture. They sat, cross-legged, in silence before entering a meditative state.

Serge focused on his breathing to eliminate any distractions. His heart rate reduced as his body relaxed. He visualised himself being a good father to Hugo and concentrated on that image. Clouds of green and orange floated in front of his eyes. His heart and his sacral chakras were open.

His breathing slowed even further. He was aware that the colour green was connected with love, compassion and acceptance and that orange was closely connected to creativity and emotional expression.

His inner voice spoke.

"You are important to Hugo, Serge. Guide him throughout his life. He needs you."

Subconsciously, he answered.

"I will. I already love him as if he was my own son."

His concentration was broken. Slowly opening his eyes, he found Hugo watching him.

Silently, Serge thanked God for sending Hugo his way. When Hugo had asked him earlier if he could call him Père, he could see that Hugo was slowly recovering.

"Père. Let's go. We have work to do."

Hugo's heart swelled with joy. Hugo had just called him Père!

"Ok son. We'll go now."

Father and son strolled out of the labyrinth, along the meditation path and across the stream.

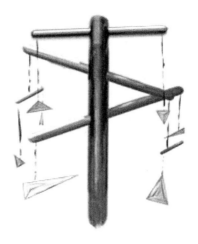

CHAPTER THIRTY SEVEN

Sleep evaded Hugo. He stretched over onto the bedside table for his laptop and quickly typed in his password.

Since he'd updated the computer earlier in the week with a new software package, he'd been experiencing problems with the operating system.

He clicked the mouse and started to navigate his way around the several icons on his desktop. His aptitude for intense detail and his unwavering ability to continue working until a problem was solved, was just one of the positive attributes of his autism.

His thirst for knowledge was another!

After a full hour of flitting in and out of the settings icon and internet channels, he clicked onto a different search engine to gather information on famous sculptors. He located some details about the renowned British sculptor, Anthony Gormley.

Success! He'd managed to clear the computer glitch.

Remembering a few of his previous discussions with Serge, he recalled the way Gormley captures the theme of identity and the relationship with others in his art forms. He really admired his style. It was significant for the piece of work he had in mind.

His decision was made. He didn't want to erect a headstone for his mother's resting place. He wanted to design a sculpture which he would site in her garden, between the flowers that she loved to tend. He would bury her ashes beside it. Then, she'd always be near him!

An image of her instantly came into his mind. She was cutting flowers and placing them into a basket. Waves of sadness surrounded him and the recurring emptiness gnawed and scratched at his stomach.

Crouching over, he tried to ease his pain. It was an acute physical and mental pain, which left him feeling weak. His heart ached. He missed her terribly.

After a short while the pain began to ease. He picked up his pencil and sketched two simple images.

Feeling sleepy, he put down his pencil and switched off his laptop.

He lay down. He knew which type of sculpture he wanted to create. It would be a simple one. The one where he was leaning against his precious mother.

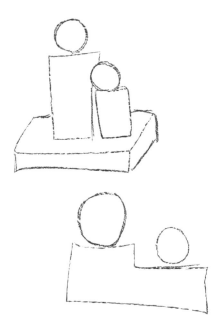

In a way he'd leant on her all his life and she had, unconditionally, loved him and nurtured him, in spite of his differences. She'd defended him when others had criticised his autistic traits. Only she could unravel his numerous idiosyncrasies and rationalise them.

Allowing sleep to overcome him, he closed his eyes and pulled the bed covers over him.

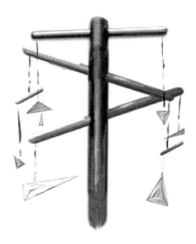

CHAPTER THIRTY EIGHT

Over breakfast, Hugo and Serge discussed designs for Nicole's sculpture.

"These are two sketches which I did during the night. I couldn't sleep."

Serge studied both of the rough sketches and he immediately knew which one Hugo had chosen.

"The one of you leaning against your maman is particularly poignant, Hugo."

"I know. That is the one I want to create. It says everything about how she was with me."

Between eating, Hugo questioned Serge

about the processes and the materials he would need. He wanted to know everything in detail.

Serge obliged him.

"Would you like to go to the quarry today? We can choose some stone. We could go now if you like."

No reply was necessary. Without any hesitation, Hugo commenced clearing the breakfast table. Tremors of excitement spread through his limbs, making him feel slightly weak and shaky.

Serge watched him and smiled.

"I'll need to go and clear out the van, if we are to bring some stone back with us."

Emptying the van, Serge pondered on how his fatherly role had evolved and the way in which Hugo had confided in him and trusted him. It had started the first time he'd met him and learnt about his autism. He'd wanted to protect him then and teach him about life and survival – and art! He'd do everything in his power to encourage and develop him in many ways.

Returning to the house, Serge noticed that Hugo was eagerly waiting for him; his bag slung over his shoulder, ready to leave.

Even though it was only one hour's drive to Montpellier, Hugo had prepared some cheese baguettes and packed several bottles of water for the journey.

"Come, Père. Let's go."

Serge locked the door and they both walked, side by side, to the van.

During the journey, Hugo talked incessantly about what he wanted to create. He repeatedly asked questions about the types of marble and stone he'd need and the techniques involved in the sculpting process. Excitement building and eager to articulate his vision, he wanted to know about everything!

Serge patiently repeated the procedures until Hugo had grasped every aspect. He was sure that whatever Hugo created, it would be a splendid piece of art. His fixation with perfection was so compelling that the finished piece of art would be spectacular.

On arrival at the quarry, they were greeted by the manager, Pierre. Serge had rang him earlier to say that they'd be visiting.

Pierre guided them to a section of the quarry where he had chosen several pieces of marble for them to look at.

Seven pieces of marble were placed side by side, ready for close inspection. Some pieces of the metamorphic rock contained swirls and others had elongated, grey meandering lines of varying widths, running through them. The organic pieces of rock were natural pieces of art in themselves, without any sculptor's hand ever having touched them.

Hugo imagined which pieces he would use for his sculpture. He looked at three specific pieces. He needed one for the base and two chunks for the sculptures of himself and his mother.

"Père. I like these three pieces. I think

they're the right shape. What do you think?"

"Which pieces are you intending to use for the figurative forms?"

Hugo pointed to two taller and slender pieces.

"If you are intent on portraying yourself in the sculpture as a child, you really don't need two of the same size."

"Ah! Yes! Which one do you think would be more suitable, then?"

Serge chose a smaller, thicker chunk of stone which had several finer veins running through it. It somehow seemed very life-like and was the ideal shape to be sculpted into the image of a young boy.

"This one would be ideal for what you want to portray, Hugo. It is a fine piece."

"Yes. I will have that one then. Is the other one okay for my maman? Do you think this one is okay for the base?"

"Yes, the other two are suitable, Hugo. The base needs to be oblong and the right dimensions to take both sculptures, so you have chosen well."

Pierre observed from a distance. He had done business with Serge for many years and admired his expertise and technique; the way he could cleverly construct excellent pieces of artwork out of rough pieces of stone.

They surveyed the slabs of stone, nodding in agreement. Serge placed his right hand on Hugo's shoulder as he advised him on the different types of stone.

"The pure-white marble is so much easier to carve into, Hugo. As a novice, you will find it easy to work with, because it's likely to shatter when you start chipping away at it. This type of marble is also more weather-resistant and so it'll be suitable for placing in the garden."

Pierre had recognised a significant change in Serge. The gloomy grey cloak of sadness which he'd worn for years, even after his marriage to Suzette, was now removed and, in its place, was a bright blue aura. Serge seemed much calmer; more contented. The sensitive, fatherly manner he displayed towards Hugo caused Pierre to smile, as he subtly detected the magnetic energy-field which vibrated steadily around Serge's body.

He approached them both.

"Have you chosen some suitable pieces for your sculptures, Hugo?"

"Yes. I have Pierre. I would like to take these three slabs please. How much do I owe you?"

Serge interrupted and nodded towards Pierre.

"Place these on my account please. He's going to need his own set of tools, so he can start on his sculpture right away. You know the brand I use."

Pierre bowed his head in acknowledgement and walked back towards his office.

"Père. I have money to buy the stone.

Allow me to pay for it."

Serge place his hand on Hugo's left shoulder.

"Please accept my gift, Hugo. I'm delighted that you are interested in creating a sculpture. My own father bought me my first set of tools and slabs of marble and I would like to do the same for you."

"Merci. Père. I'm most grateful."

As the chunks of marble were too heavy to go into the van, Serge decided to take just one piece. The other pieces would be delivered the following day. Work could commence on one of the figures, whilst they were waiting for the others to arrive.

With the tools and marble placed securely within the van, they headed back to Lezignan, stopping on the way to eat their lunch under the shade of some walnut trees on the canal bank.

"Père, I'm very excited about creating my sculpture. Can we start on it this afternoon?"

"Yes. We can start the preparation process, but we'll need to wait for the other slabs to arrive tomorrow and then we can plan the design."

After eating, they continued with their short journey, arriving back home in the mid- afternoon.

Serge parked the car just outside his studio. They could just about manage to carry the marble slab between them, without using the portable hoist. He gave Hugo a pair of gloves and put on his own gloves.

"Put these gloves on, Hugo. They'll protect the surface of the marble as we carry it."

Together they cautiously moved the slab into the studio, siting it just inside the tall sliding doors.

Hugo stood back to admire the slab, imagining the figurative shape that he would soon carve.

"Get your sketches, Hugo. We'll need to take some measurements and make further sketches before we start. We can then begin the marking out process."

Hugo returned with his sketches and the two of them worked until early evening preparing the slab.

A willing student, Hugo listened intently to Serge's instructions, making copious drawings and notes to remind himself of the different stages.

After a meal of tagliatelle pasta with trout and some home-made rhubarb ice-cream, they sat in relative silence on the kitchen terrace, gazing at the breathtakingly-beautiful sunset disappearing below the horizon.

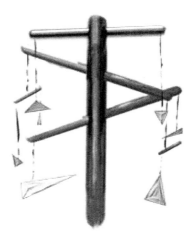

CHAPTER THIRTY NINE

Much was learnt over the days that followed; not only creative skills, but life skills also.

Hugo inspected the blocks of marble being carefully unloaded; his facial expressions revealing his enthusiasm.

After their delivery into the studio, Hugo and Serge started shaping the base of the sculpture. The slab would be positioned in the garden first and then the other two sculptures would be slotted into it, after they had been completed.

Serge re-examined each piece individually,

carefully looking for fractures that would impact the shape of the sculpture. It was as perfect as the day they had viewed it in the quarry.

Hugo was a quick learner. He absorbed every detail and instruction that Serge proffered. He became aware of the health and safety aspects involved when working with marble; making sure that he wore the correct clothing and used the correct tools for each part of the creation.

"Allow the sculpture to speak to you, Hugo. It will guide you to the shape it wants to be. Treat the marble with respect. Engage with its human aspects. Imagine its personality."

Hugo's creativity soared as he recollected his close relationship with his mother. With hammer and chisel, he chipped away, capturing the physical and emotional sensations whilst he eliminated the unwanted areas. He'd already decided that he wanted the sculpted image of her to be smooth. He didn't want a textured finish.

The teacher observed the student closely and was amazed at his apprentice's newly-learnt skills and his direct, personal encounter with the slab. Hugo's hand movements were exacting as he used a flat chisel to finely shape the slightly-contoured waist from the block of marble; which was slowly transforming into an abstract image of Nicole.

For a novice, Hugo already had an excellent, conceptual eye for shape and technique. He had the ability and the willingness to learn new skills.

Serge felt proud of Hugo's determination. He was reminded of his younger self, when his father would instruct him on the traditional and crucial techniques. Carving had become a constant in his life and one that would remain with him until the end of his days on earth.

The balanced ventilation system, humming contentedly in the background, played a soothing symphony as Hugo donned his ultra-thin gloves and carried out the smoothing process under Serge's guidance.

Adjusting the full dust-mask and visor which covered his face, he picked up a bottle of water and quenched his thirst. He knew he shouldn't allow himself to become dehydrated.

"Père. I can't wait to finish it", he enthused.

Serge grinned at his eagerness and offered several words of advice.

"You cannot hurry your creation, Hugo. It takes time, technique, dedication and patience to complete a unique piece of art."

"But, I want to see it finished, Père ."

"If you rush, you may crack the piece of marble and your carving will then be ruined. It sometimes happens, even to the expert carvers, when the point of the chisel unintentionally hits a natural seam. Carving is a gradual game of patience. You have to wait and see what transpires."

Hugo moved his neck from side to side, trying to release some tension which had built up in his upper arms and shoulders. He hadn't envisaged the physical demands that aesthetic carving would bring.

Serge was aware of Hugo's exhaustion. He was also acutely aware that a substantial amount of tension was necessary to channel the excessive force of the hammer onto the chisel.

"Embrace every single stage of the process; the resistance, the total respect it commands and the energy it demands."

Cautiously, Hugo continued at a much slower pace. His shoulders, still aching, were taut as he attempted to set free the abstract figure of his mother, that was temporarily confined within the partly-transformed block of marble. As Serge had advised, he allowed the sculpture to speak to him and gently guide him towards the areas which needed to be removed. An unexpected human relationship with the marble was being formed.

From a distance, Serge continued to monitor Hugo's fatigue.

"Come now, Hugo. It's time to finish. We must eat. It's getting late."

"I need to tidy up after myself, Père. I can't leave all this mess."

"It's okay, Hugo. I'll help you in the morning."

Not wanting to go, he relented and took off his visor and gloves. Standing back, he admired his work in progress, fascinated with his efforts.

The critical and dedicated attention he'd

given to his work had totally wiped his energy; but not his enthusiasm. He couldn't wait to continue with it the following day!

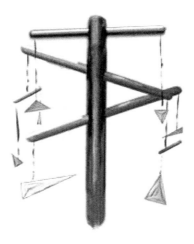

CHAPTER FORTY

Seven days after arriving in Liverpool, Suzette was seated on the early morning flight to Carcassonne, accompanied by her niece, Sarah.

During her stay, she had visited her relatives and had invited Sarah to come back to France with her for a two-week holiday.

Sarah had jumped at the chance; promptly booking her plane tickets and stuffing clothes into her suitcase.

The plane's shuddering touchdown in Carcassonne startled Sarah; even though Suzette had previously warned her of the short runway.

She had soon forgotten the scary experience as she descended the steps and was welcomed by the brilliant sunshine and the warm Mediterranean breeze.

Serge and Hugo were waiting in the arrivals area. After embracing her husband and Hugo, Suzette introduced Sarah to Hugo. They collected their luggage and walked over to the car.

After a short journey through the centre of Carcassonne, they took a left turn into the village of Trebes. Serge wanted to buy some bread and macarons from his favourite patisserie.

Whilst driving home through the winding, country lanes on their way back to Lezignan, Serge and Suzette and Serge discussed her visit to England. The conversation between Hugo and Sarah was limited. Although he spoke good English and Sarah spoke a little French, Hugo was lost for words and Sarah, fully aware of his recent loss, respected his silence. She was happy to admire the impressive landscapes and the endless rows of grapevines on either side of her.

After arriving home, Hugo directed Sarah to her room, next to his at the rear of the house, before leaving her to do her unpacking.

Over a light lunch on the kitchen terrace, Serge relayed what had been happening whilst Suzette had been away.

On this occasion, Hugo was eager to join in the conversation.

"Suzette, I'm so excited. With Père's, I

mean Serge's help, I'm creating a sculpture for my maman's garden. It's not finished yet, but when I have completed it, I'll show you."

Suzette was impressed by the change in Hugo and she smiled when he referred to Serge as his père.

Serge raised his eyebrows and returned her smile.

Sarah still felt a little uncomfortable in Hugo's presence, although she was intrigued as to how his sculpture would look. She was also intrigued with his handsome looks and enigmatic persona.

Subtly, Suzette brought Sarah into the conversation.

"Sarah's an holistic therapist, Hugo. She's built herself a good reputation. Sports people and even some senior medical practitioners go to her for treatment."

"Really? I don't know much about holistic therapy. What is it?" enquired Hugo.

Serge listened intently. Maybe some therapies may help Hugo.

"I treat the client as a whole. Rather than just treating the body, I'm also concerned with their spirit. I qualified five years ago and I have a private practice within a health club. I also lecture students in a local training centre."

"You should have been here a few weeks ago, when Suzette was delivering one of her courses. I'm sure that your therapies would have alleviated some of the anxiety and stress that we were all experiencing at the time."

Sarah agreed with him. Her complementary therapies encouraged the body to heal itself by boosting the immune system.

"I'm sure they would have, Serge".

Suzette cleared the table and went inside, leaving the others to continue with the discussion.

On her return to the kitchen terrace, she heard Serge telling Sarah about the labyrinth.

"Would you like to see it, Sarah?" she asked. "Yes. I would. I'm very interested. You spoke a little about it when we were on the plane. Is it possible to go there now?"

"Of course. I've missed my daily meditation sessions there, whilst I've been away."

Hugo and Serge, eager to return to the studio to work on the sculpture, left Suzette and Sarah to meander over to the clearing and the labyrinth.

CHAPTER FORTY ONE

During dinner that evening, the conversation was as diverse as the food they ate.

Before moving into the house to eat, they'd sat under the branches of the fig trees, nibbling small slices of fresh fig and ricotta crostini; a chilled bottle of Blanquette de Limoux close by, to keep them company.

Sarah had been inspired by the labyrinth and didn't want to leave it.

"I felt as if I was in a sacred place. It was so ethereal. I was very relaxed there. I could actually feel the stresses draining away from my body", she gushed as she lifted the flute of sparkling wine to her mouth.

Hugo, now feeling more confident around Sarah, interjected.

"Me, too. It was like I was in another world. A world where you felt protected and safe. Since my maman died, I go there every day. It helps me."

Suzette interrupted the conversation. She was ready to serve the starter.

They moved inside and sat around the dining table. Suzette served them with a slice of prawn and trout terrine, garnished with basil and lemon shreds and on a side plate there were thin slices of walnut bread.

Tucking in, sounds of appreciation could be heard as the terrine melted in their mouths.

"Mmm. C'est tellement délicieux Suzette. C'est la meilleure terrine que j'ai goûtée", declared Hugo.

"I agree with you, Hugo. It is the best terrine I have tasted too. Suzette serves some outstanding food", Serge enthused.

Silence followed until the plates were empty.

"Is your sculpture nearing completion, Hugo?" asked Suzette.

"Almost. I'm in the final stages. Earlier, I've been polishing each piece to bring out the colours. It's a slow, but satisfying, process. Serge has taught me endless techniques."

"Each piece, Hugo." I thought there was

only one sculpture."

Serge leant back in his chair as Hugo intricately explained the structure of his design.

"Once it's completed, it will be one piece. At the moment it consists of three pieces and it will be assembled together when I've finished it. I am only a novice and to carve the sculpture out of one chunk of stone would have been too difficult for me."

Serge nodded in agreement, silently endorsing his honest admission.

"It was challenging, but I think I've managed to do a good job. With Serge's expert guidance and much patience, I'm satisfied with my first attempt."

Serge cleared the table and followed Suzette into the kitchen.

As she lifted the caramelised vegetable tarte tatin from the oven, Serge's saliva glands respected the effort she'd put into making it.

Turning the tarte out of the baking tray, the selection of vegetables on a puff pastry base, were randomly charred with a caramelised topping.

Serge took charge, slicing even oblongs of tarte and placing them onto the white porcelain platters, just off centre.

Suzette placed a small amount of fresh fig and goat's cheese salad alongside it, before garnishing the top with walnuts, leaving the remainder of the salad in the bowl for extra helpings.

The portions of gastronomic art were

placed before Sarah and Hugo, along with a newly-opened bottle of wine.

"This looks interesting, Auntie Suze", declared Sarah.

"I'm sure you'll like it."

The main course was devoured, as was the remaining bowl of salad.

Suzette directed her question to Hugo and Serge.

"Are you going to be working on the sculpture tomorrow? I think I'll take Sarah for a tour of the region after breakfast."

"Yes. We're aiming to complete it within the next few days and then we can erect it in Nicole's garden at the weekend. You don't mind do you?" replied Serge.

"Not at all. It'll be an opportunity for Sarah to see the picturesque, Languedoc landscapes."

"I would really love that. I've already read up on the Languedoc Roussillon and the medieval culture which is still in existence in some of the older settlements. Can we visit some castles and maybe go to Sète and Banyuls and Gruissan and that place that sounds like the last tours?"

Suzette laughed at her pronunciation.

"I presume you are speaking about Lastours, Sarah."

"Yes, I think that's what it's called. I remember reading that there are four castle ruins there. That Simon de Montfort was a ruthless and brutal man. I read all about how he sadistically slaughtered masses of people in the Cathar wars, just because they wouldn't convert to his Catholic religion. If he was supposed to be a man of God, then why was he so intent on persecuting people?"

"Religion has a lot to answer for. Montfort failed miserably though. His terror tactics didn't work at Lastours. He repeatedly failed to capture the castles. The rugged landscape would've made travelling difficult in those times and the steep location of the castles would have enabled those inside to easily spot their enemies approaching", interjected Hugo.

"We can go there, Sarah, but you'll need to be prepared for trundling over uneven ground and climbing up endless steps to reach the high rocks."

"I don't mind. Honestly. I'd love to explore the ruins and imagine what life would have been like in those days."

"Ok. We'll need to leave early, though. It'll be too hot to be walking and climbing in the midday heat", advised Suzette.

Clearing the table once more, Serge withdrew to the kitchen to collect the dessert.

The wide glass bowls, filled with coconut, mint and mango parfait, were retrieved from the fridge and sprinkled with chards of dark chocolate, before Serge returned to the others.

Suzette slid her spoon into the smooth puree mixture and let the dense, silky texture melt on her tongue. Her taste receptors reeled from its sheer piquancy. She loved the bizarre combination of the ingredients. Serge was a connoisseur when it came to making desserts. He had such a sweet tooth, as did she!

"This is luscious, darling."

"I agree", he retorted as he flashed his eyes in her direction.

After drinking coffee and peppermint tea, they ended the evening with a small glass of rhubarb and ginger liqueur before retreating to their beds.

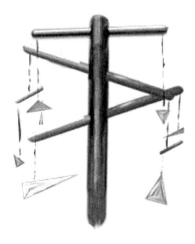

CHAPTER FORTY TWO

The smoothing process revealed the intricate, grey lines which had been partly visible on the marble when they'd first seen it. The translucent sheen was exquisite and, with each meticulous polish, the geometric figures appeared to come to life.

Hugo's distinctive and deeply-personal encounter with the assumed, humanistic shapes had only served to reinforce his profound feelings for his maman. Although there were no features in his sculptures, his personal abstraction of her revealed her character and was indicative of her strength. The petite, yet perfectly-formed circle depicting her face, seemed to smile at him. How convenient that the asymmetrical veining in the marble happened to be in that precise part of the slab.   The straightened edges, representing the broad shoulders, represented her intense fortitude during her most challenging periods. The squareness of it reminded him of her ethical stance on life, before illness had cruelly invaded her body.

His own depiction of himself as a child was also poignant. He'd deftly positioned the smaller figure leaning into the larger one, with its head tilted upwards in admiration and love.

Hugo's venture into sculptural, abstraction had proved to be demanding as well as fulfilling. The purposeful channelling of his acute pain into the three chunks of marble, had been therapeutic.

Serge had remained at the labyrinth after they had meditated earlier; tending to the plants and tidying the area surrounding the summer house.

Hugo removed his gloves. He didn't want to overwork the pieces; being mindful of his obsessive craving to perfect his work. As he was clearing his tools away, he became aware of Serge's presence at the other end of the studio.

"So, you've completed your masterpiece then, Hugo."

Hugo shrugged his shoulders and exhaled; his loud breath indicating the energy he had recently expended.

"I think so, Père. Will you examine it and

give your opinion?"

Serge walked around each piece, examining each in detail. He was amazed at the exceptionality of the skills which were presented before him. Hugo's highly-functioning, autistic attributes had infiltrated the human-like abstractions, conveying an enigmatic identity to the figurative sculptures.

Hugo waited for Serge's response.   None was forthcoming; other than several nods of the head and a folding of hands.

Serge stopped at the smaller sculpture and he inspected the positioning of it against the larger one. He allowed his emotions to surface, knowing what the sculpture represented. Whatever Hugo (supposedly) lacked in social misinterpretation, he compensated for it with his creative imagination and his totally unwavering resolve to complete his personal project.

Contrary   to   what   educationalists   think about   people   with   autism,   Hugo's   abstract interpretation of his mother and himself, certainly challenged their theories that the autistic person's learning should be of a 'concrete' nature. Some theorists also maintain that difficult tasks should be avoided because they demotivate and frustrate; another highly arguable viewpoint!

Hugo had focused the depth of his feelings into his art. The repetitive motions in completing the task had been advantageous in this instance.

Serge smiled at Hugo, who was waiting for a verdict on his creation. Contemplating the recent

SUSAN M HIGGINS

events, Serge speculated whether all humans could be deemed to be at some point on the autistic scale.   In fact, his own mannerisms could be interpreted as bordering on the compulsive and obsessive. Other individuals he'd been acquainted with, also displayed idiosyncrasies and numerous eccentric attributes; all of which were considered to be 'normal'. Whatever normal is supposed to be!

"Well. Père. Does my work please you?"

"Of course. It pleases me very much, Hugo. Exceptionnel! Magnifique! Spectaculaire!

"Merci, Père. I'm pleased that you like it."

Serge approached Hugo. He firmly placed his arm on the young man's shoulder.

"I spoke to the sculptures, like you said, Père. I imagined they were human beings. I explored the possibility of them being spirits. I believe I've actually transferred my own spirit and that of my maman into them."

"Whatever you did, Hugo, you have produced a very impressive piece of art. Now, all we have to do is assemble it and erect it in your garden. We can do it on Saturday."

Nicole's passing had been an opportunity for self-growth for both of them.

That night, Hugo wrote in his journal.

'Tu me manques Maman. Veille sur moi.'

He was sure that his maman missed him too and that she was always watching over him!

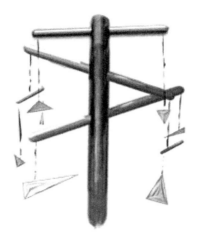

CHAPTER FORTY THREE

Over the days that followed, Suzette and Sarah spent much of their time visiting places of interest and shopping at the local markets, whilst Serge and Hugo prepared the garden for Nicole's sculpture.

On each of their excursions to Lastours and Carcassonne, Sarah felt as if she'd time-travelled. History seeped out of the walls of the imposing castles. From both battlements she could see the snow on top of the Pyrenees and the stunning views of the sprawling Languedoc countryside.

She'd also enjoyed rummaging amongst the market stalls in Narbonne and Luecate. There was no need to buy any lunch. Tasting the numerous free samples of olives, tapanades, cheeses, sun-dried tomatoes and various nuts had amply satisfied her hunger.

Meanwhile, Hugo and Serge had cleared a piece of land outside the full-length doors, near the rear of the house. They'd poured a concrete base onto a thick layer of compacted gravel, to take the full weight of the sculpture. The finished pieces had been transported across in the van, ready to be assembled.

On Saturday morning, the four of them helped to erect the masterpiece.

Suzette and Sarah guided Serge as he steered the larger piece into a groove on the marble base. It fitted perfectly with no movement detected.

Hugo lifted the smaller piece and placed it into the slot alongside it. The precision of its position was amazingly accurate, with the imagined head resting on the shoulders of the larger one.

The marble abstract images of mother and son dazzled under the rays of the late morning sun; a permanent reminder of the staunch dedication and love a mother had for her son.

As they toasted Nicole with glasses of sparking wine and ate lunch amongst the wildflowers and fruit trees, a blue butterfly gently danced around the table before landing on the figurative carving.

Message received! The visitor's identity was

acknowledged as they lifted their glasses once more!

All would be okay.

CHAPTER FORTY FOUR

The telephone rang. Suzette rushed inside to answer it. She was expecting a call from her son who lived in Sardinia. He'd gone out there with his job as lifestyle researcher linked to a UK healthy living project two years ago; taking along his young family with him. He'd previously accomplished a similar wellbeing project in Sweden.

The healthy lifestyle and climate suited him as he was fanatical in his strive to remain healthy.

A little disappointed that the call was not from her son, she must have sounded a little impolite to the caller who wanted to speak to

Serge.

"Oh! I was expecting another call. I'll just get him. Who's calling please?"

The caller answered her in a fractured English accent.

"It's the manager at the Museum of Modern Art in Collioure."

"One moment, please."

Suzette found Serge clearing out some fallen leaves from the stream.

"Darling. There's a call for you. The manager of the museum in Collioure would like to speak with you. Come quickly."

He wiped his hands on the sides of his shorts and followed Suzette inside.

Serge introduced himself and listened intently as the called explained that he had a client who was interested in one of his sculptures. It was the one with the two hollow pieces which he'd sculpted ten years ago. The one which held special memories for him; albeit a poignant portrayal of a sad time in his life.

Suzette moved closer, in an effort to decipher the content of the conversation.

She deduced that someone wanted to buy one of his pieces and that the prospective buyer wanted to meet him the following day to discuss the possibility of a sale.

Serge pondered on the possibility of selling his sculpture and agreed wo meet up with the buyer. The manager had told him that she was very keen on buying several other pieces of artwork from the museum and was enthusiastic about the meeting. He would be; the museum would collect a hefty fee from the sale!

Suzette was intrigued as Serge ended the call.

His furrowed brow creased as he raised his eyebrows and rubbed his forehead.

"Someone wants to buy one of my sculptures. I've just arranged to meet a Sardinian woman, Madame Nazzari, at noon tomorrow in Collioure."

"Oh! Which sculpture is it?"

"It's the one which is the representation of myself with the hollow spaces."

Suzette recalled the first time she'd seen it.

"Do you think you'll sell it to her?"

"I'll have to talk with her first. I'm interested to see why she's attracted to it. I don't really know whether I will, Suzette. We'll go along tomorrow and see what transpires."

Serge returned to complete his work at the stream. He reflected on the period when he'd created his masterpiece. He'd spent many long hours deliberating on the design and crafting it. The sculpture depicted his melancholic mood. The hollow spaces, within the body of the figurative image, represented the abject emptiness of how he'd felt.

Suzette ruminated on the conversation. One minute she'd been expecting a call from her son in Sardinia and then Serge receives a telephone call about a Sardinian woman.

As her intuition acknowledged the meaningful, synchronistic communication, she had a strong gut feeling that the random encounter would produce a significant outcome.

The phone rang again. This time she knew that it *was* her son!

"Hello, Mum. How are you? I've been trying to get you. Is there a problem with your phone?"

"Hello, Alex. I'm good thanks. No. Serge had an impromptu call that he needed to take.

The conversation centred around his family and his job. The project was going very well and he'd learnt a lot about the longevity and the habits of the people who lived there.

He loved his job. It was a healthier lifestyle for him, his wife and his two children. The yearly results influenced advocacy groups, government policies and, hopefully in the near future, would change the lifestyles of people in England.

"So everyone's okay, then, Alex. How are Albert and Clio and Annie."

"Yes, Mum. We're all okay. I'll ring you soon. Take care. Bye, Mum. Love you."

"You take care too, son. Good to speak with you. Love you too. Bye"

After ending the call, Suzette's feelings were mixed; happy that she'd spoken with him and sad that she hadn't seen him for a while.

She'd only seen him an handful of times since he'd left England. She missed him, terribly!

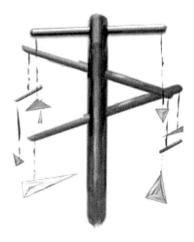

CHAPTER FORTY FIVE

They arrived at Collioure at 11.30am. After parking the van, they strolled through the narrow, cobbled streets and made the way towards the Museum.

Yesterday, whilst at the labyrinth, Serge had pondered over the telephone discussion and the forthcoming appointment with Madame Nazzari. Depending on how their conversation progressed, he thought that he may possibly sell the sculpture to her. It was definitely one of his élite pieces! His finest pieces were, almost always, the ones he'd produced during his moments of adversity.

The concierge welcomed them and directed

them to a private room where Madam Nazzari was waiting. She arose as they entered the room and offered her hand to Serge and then to Suzette.

"Bonjour. I'm so glad you agreed to meet me", she intonated with a hint of sadness in her voice.

"Bonjour, Madame Nazzari. So you like my carving, then? Have you viewed any of my other work?"

She nodded.

"Actually, I have. My late husband loved your work. He had business contacts in America. He'd seen several pieces of your work. Someone told me that you had some of your sculptures displayed here in Collioure and, as I was holidaying in the South of France, I made a detour to view them."

"I do believe you are interested in the figurative carving. The one with the hollow piercings?"

"I am. I can't really say why I'm drawn to it, other than it oozes an equal amount of sadness and love. It somehow reminds me of my husband. He'd wanted to commission you before he died, but we never did get around to making contact with you."

Suzette raised her eyebrows. She observed Serge's reaction.

"Monsieur Couture, would it be rude of me to ask if you identified yourself with this piece? I'm aware that emotion is crucial when creating any obscure piece of art."

Suzette gasped as Serge composed himself before answering. It was as if Madame Nazzari was interpreting his intense, emotional involvement with the abstract form.

"My work is meant to be enigmatic and, yet, *you* can read it perfectly. Most spectators walk past, unable to decipher its relevance."

"Ah! I sensed its relevance the moment I saw it. I was transfixed with how the empty spaces conveyed the truth. They revealed the powerful elements of a human's anguish and devotion."

Serge was speechless. This complete stranger was somehow reading him. How could she sense the extreme emotional state he was in when he'd created the figure?

Not knowing how to react to her accurate interpretation, he moved closer to Suzette for support.

"Have I alarmed you, Monsieur Couture? I'm so sorry if I have. I'm merely stating what I am sensing in your work. It is an outstanding piece of art. My late husband would've loved it. I love it! Are you willing to sell me it?"

After listening to her thorough appraisal of his figurative piece and her forthright approach, he'd made his decision.

After a brief negotiation over lunch, the deal was done; the fee instantly transferred and cleared in Serge's bank.

On first name terms now, Suzette liked this

woman. Caterina's insightful, clairsentient abilities were not too dissimilar to her own skills. Caterina had extended an invitation for them to go over to Sardinia and see the sculpture installed in her home.

Suzette's mind was working overtime as she imagined combining the visit to Caterina with a visit to her son and his family.

"We would like that, Caterina. We'd like it very much. Thank you for your offer."

"As soon as I have arranged for it to be sited in our atrium, I will contact you."

Serge had offered to arrange shipment of the sculpture, but Caterina preferred to use her own trusted carriers, who would ensure it was delivered safely.

"I would be very grateful though, if you could supervise the packing and removal of it into the container. I've acquired some other large pieces that will also be included in the same shipment."

"I'll give you my guarantee that I'll personally oversee the packing for you, Caterina."

After saying farewell, Caterina's handsome chauffeur took her by the hand and escorted her to a waiting car.

Before leaving, Serge liaised with the manager, giving him strict instructions to contact him when the carrier was due to collect it.

They travelled in silence for most of the way home. Suzette knew that Serge would feel some sadness at having sold his sculpture, especially as its significance was related to earlier events in his life.

"How are you feeling, Serge?"

"Surprisingly, I'm feeling happy. I know that Caterina will appreciate it. The carving is part of my past. I've realised that it's not healthy for me to be too precious about my material possessions. I'm just happy that other individuals will gain some pleasure from looking at it."

Suzette reached over and kissed his cheek.

"Hey, Monsieur Couture. Have you been on one of those self-development courses?"

He nodded.

They both laughed heartily and continued to laugh, intermittently, until they reached home.

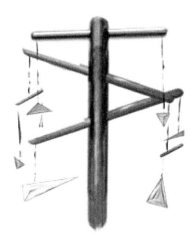

CHAPTER FORTY SIX

Removal of his sculpture happened quickly. The museum telephoned the following day and, with Serge's expert supervision, the shipment occurred two days later.

Whilst eating dinner with Sarah and Hugo that evening, they spoke about travelling to Sardinia to see Alex and his family.

"I'm a little concerned about leaving you on your own, Hugo."

"It's ok. I'll be fine, Père. I have to take some responsibility for my own life."

Sarah joined in the conversation.

"Yes. Please go and enjoy yourselves. I was going to ask you if I could stay a while longer. I love it here. I don't want to go back, yet."

Sarah and Hugo had become more friendly. They'd been renovating the house and working in the garden, spending most of their days together.

At first, Sarah had found it difficult to interpret his silent moments and his periods of solitude. He was rigid in his routine, whilst she was flexible. When Hugo didn't respond immediately to her questions, she'd continue asking him if he had understood her; sometimes raising her voice in case he hadn't heard her. He'd heard her perfectly the first time, but he just needed some time to process the information before he gave her his answer. He felt nervous in case he gave her the wrong answer, or if he didn't give her the answer he thought she may have wanted to hear.

On a few rare occasions, he'd plucked up the courage to explain to her about his needs and how he reacted if things didn't go to plan.

She learned not to ask too many questions at once. She learned that he may not get the gist of what she was saying. She learned that he may take what she said literally. She learned to accept his differences. She learned patience. She learnt that he was better with routine. Sarah learned lots of things, quickly!

Hugo fixated on things. He had a fixation with the labyrinth, a fixation with sculptures and how marble was formed from the chemicals within the earth. He also had a fixation with everything being in the right place. He had difficulty with change, but he was learning to adapt his ways, with the Sarah's help.

Sarah found his behaviour challenging and yet, she found herself falling into his way of living. She was also falling for his sensitive nature and his ability to make her laugh for no reason.

Suzette was concerned about Sarah's business in England.

"What about your work, Sarah? "

"I was just waiting to see what you said first, before I rang home."

"Of course, you can stay. Stay as long as you like, but you must remember that you do have responsibilities at home."

"I know. But it feels right, being here with you all."

Serge and Suzette had witnessed a change in Hugo since Sarah had arrived almost two weeks ago. They'd also noticed that the two of them had their own unique way of communicating. They used gestures and signs. Occasionally, they would use single words or write short notes to each other.

"Well, if that's what you want, Sarah. You know your own mind", Serge reaffirmed.

"Thank you Auntie Suze. Thanks Uncle Serge. I'll ring my clients tomorrow ."

Hugo courageously clasped her hand under the table. He was a bit frightened that she might reject him, but she didn't. It felt good!

Sarah had been flirting with him for the past week. She thought he hadn't read her signals.

Obviously, he had!

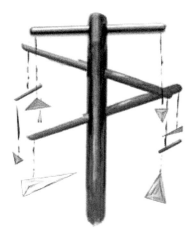

CHAPTER FORTY SEVEN

Telephone calls had been made, the flights had been booked, lists had been left for Hugo and Sarah and luggage had been packed.

The journey to Acciaroli was long, but well worth it to be with their family. On the five hour flight, they ate, read, drank and snoozed.

The plane landed in Naples early in the afternoon and Alex was waiting for them in the arrivals area.

Suzette rushed over to him and hugged him.

"It's been too long, son. I've missed you."

"I've missed you too, Mum. Bonjour Serge."

He embraced Serge before making their way over to the car park. Their journey would take around two hours, covering eighty five miles; but they should easily manage to miss the evening traffic, if they were able to navigate their way through Naples successfully.

"How's your work, Alex?" enquired Serge.

"It's great. I love it. I love the village, the people and the lifestyle. I don't ever want to leave here and go back to live a stressful lifestyle in England. It's good for the children and Annie, too."

"How many other countries are involved in the project with you?" asked Suzette.

"There are several, Mum. Everyone is eager to find the secrets to longevity. Do you know that one third of the population is over one hundred years old. They're healthy and happy and stress free! There are people in their late nineties who are still working. They even ride their bikes to work. It's so amazing to see them."

"How interesting!"

Alex steered the car along the motorway lanes, past beautiful landscaped mountains and coastlines. The air felt fresh and unpolluted. There didn't seem to be that many cars on the roads. Some shepherds could be seen strolling in the rural shrubland and surrounding hills, tending to their sheep. They, too, looked as if they were in the super-age category with their weathered skins, slightly-hunched backs and walking canes.

On reaching the village, several older women in their pinnies were sitting outside their front doors on faded, wooden chairs, watching children playing in the street. Outside most of the bars, the male elders sat chatting in their white, singlet vests drinking coffee and dark red wine. Several were smoking cigarettes and were overweight.

Suzette was puzzled.

"Alex. It really makes me wonder how they've managed to live so long if they are still smoking and drinking. I presume they go to the bars every day."

"That's what we're researching, Mum. Yes they go there every day to meet their friends and chat. Social interaction is part of their lifestyle. They make up and follow their own rules here. Carnivals and other events are held in the village and everyone takes part in the dressing up and organising the food and drink. It's a traditional family way of living. It works for them; and it works for me too."

"I can see it does, Alex. Do you still exercise every day?"

"Of course. Nothing's changed. I stick to my daily routine and then I have a treat on Sundays. It suits me. I feel so much better when I'm exercising and eating healthily. It's good for my mind too. I like to stay in control"

Alex drove into a new housing development on the outskirts of the village. There were only seven houses in the horse-shoe shaped crescent. His was the first house. Suzette's grandchildren and Annie were waiting for them in the front garden.

She choked at the sight of them. They looked so much bigger than they did when she'd facetimed them. The tears flowed as they ran to her.

"Grandmama, Grandmama. You're here. Hooray", they both screamed excitedly.

She clutched on tightly, not wanting to release them.

They broke away from her and ran over to Serge.

"Hello Grandpa Serge. We've been so excited to see you. We've been counting the sleeps until you arrived", exclaimed Albert.

He bent down and held them close.

"Have you now? Let's take a closer look at you both. You've grown so big. Albert, you're so very tall and handsome. Clio, how very beautiful you look and that's a pretty dress you're wearing."

The children started running around and jumping up and down.

Albert ran over to Suzette and grabbed her arm.

"Come, Grandmama. Come and play with us. We have giant skittles and a tent and a football net and lots of toys. Come on Grandmama."

He dragged her over to the lawn and gave her the football.

"Try to get a goal, Grandmama. I'll be goalie."

Suzette couldn't stop laughing. Whatever was she doing? She didn't even like football and here she was trying to kick the ball into the net, having so much fun, with her grandson.

"You're not that good at playing football, are you Grandmama? You can't even score any goals. I have saved every one of them."

She couldn't stop laughing, especially at Albert's comments about her football skills. Toshika had said something similar about her gaming skills.

"No, darling. I'm not. I don't really get that much practice, she chuckled. Can we just stop for a moment, I need to sit down", she replied catching her breath.

"Come on then, Grandmama. You can have a nice rest in the tent. It has some cushions in there"

He clumsily dragged her over to the miniscule tent and helped her to crawl in. It was big enough for two children, but not for an adult and a young child. Feeling claustrophobic, she felt panicky but remained in the tent for the sake of her grandson, who was so excited to play games with her.

"Do you feel better now? Albert enquired.

"Much better, Albert. Thank you."

In another part of the garden, Serge was playing skittles with Clio. He was also having trouble keeping up with the energetic, little girl. He lost several games, sometimes on purpose, although Clio was quite adept at flinging the heavy ball and knocking them down with one hit.

Serge and Suzette were so thankful when Annie brought out some juice and an array of food. They all sat around the garden table, chatting incessantly and laughing until the sun set.

Later, before going to sleep, Suzette reflected on the wonderful day she'd had and how much she missed her grandchildren. They were growing up so quickly. She was determined to make every moment count whilst she was here; making memories for them and for herself, to remind her of how very lucky she was to have them.

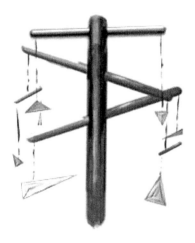

CHAPTER FORTY EIGHT

Their stay in Acciaroli, was hectic. Alex wanted to give them a tour of the surrounding areas and so their days were full, except for one particular afternoon, during the second week, when they went to visit Caterina.

Caterina had emailed Serge with directions to her humble abode. When she'd met them in Collioure, she was thrilled to hear that Suzette's son only lived a short distance from her. It was only eight miles away.

As they drove along the Strade Statale 267, the imposing blocks of multi-hued houses were like a magnificent oil painting hanging proudly over the spectacular Cilento coastline. Suzette reflected back to her schooldays in the 1960's when she'd painted a similar scene for her art exam.

Caterina's house was perched on the medieval hilltop town of Catellabate, three hundred metres above sea level. After travelling along the many winding lanes and zig-zag roads they finally arrived.

Far from being the 'humble abode' that she had implied, it was more like a castle!

Alex was searching for a door bell to announce their arrival. There was no need. A camera had spotted them driving up the hill and the electric gates opened to welcome them.

Alex followed the endless driveway, lined with rows of swaying Mediterranean palm trees, up to the front of the villa.

Caterina was waiting to greet them; equally as impressive as the stunning main entrance.

Serge's eyebrows lifted and looking towards Suzette, he cleared his throat several times.

"Well. I wasn't expecting anything like this. I actually thought that her house might be grandeur, but this is something else!"

"Yes. Something else."

Caterina warmly embraced them both and, after Suzette had politely introduced her son, Alex quickly clambered back into his car and drove off. He'd been invited in, but he'd quickly made an excuse to get away. Such extravagance, on this pointless level, didn't excite him! He'd rather be back in Acciaroli.

Inside the atrium-styled entrance stood his sculpture. He had to admit that it had been sited in a way that it was accessible from all sides; allowing the viewer to contemplate the significance of the non-representational carving. A solitary, palm tree kept it company and a luxurious velvet armchair and footstool were nearby. There was a genteel, yet peaceful, ambience to the space.

"I sit here and meditate on the days when I'm feeling sad. The panoramic view of the coastline is somewhat comforting to me. I look at the carving and imagine my husband is sat here with me. I'm a little lonely without him. He was everything to me."

Suzette could sense the extremity of her grief. She felt sorry for her and yet there was something about her words that didn't quite ring true.

Following a grand tour of the main house and grounds, they sat in a contemporary conservatory overlooking a lake, drinking wine.

"This is another favourite place of mine. I spend most days in here, listening to music and reading."

Serge was fascinated with the architectural features inside and outside of the house.

"Was this place originally a castle, Caterina?"

"Yes. It was an 18th century castle. When

we first found it, it was in ruins. My husband could instantly see its potential. He negotiated a price and took charge of its redesign and renovation. It took three years to get it to its present state.

Franco, the young man who was in Collioure with her, made an entrance. He was followed by an elderly lady in a white servant's uniform. She was navigating a heavy, glass chiller cabinet filled with delicacies and more bottles of wine.

"Signora Nazzari. Would you like me to serve you now", asked Franco.

"Yes, Franco. I'm a little hungry now and I'm sure our guests are too."

They moved over to a small dining table and Franco placed white napkins over their laps. He brought the silver platters to the table and served a selection of interesting canapes. Some were figs stuffed with mozzarella, almonds and sun-dried tomotoes. Others were tiny pieces of thinly-sliced ciabbata bread, topped with a selection of fennel and tomato puree and delicately sliced, smoked salmon topped with tiny sprigs of rosemary. A selection of stuffed and plain olives were also placed on the table.

Caterina raised her wine flute to honour her guests.

"Salute, my friends. Your good health."

Chinking each other's glasses they took a sip.

"I know that Italy is the land of the red

wine, but it's too heavy for me. I prefer white. It's more refreshing and lighter. Although, I must admit, your French wines are excellent."

Between mouthfuls of food, Serge agreed.

"We do have an excellent range of white wines in the Languedoc area. We can vouch for that!"

Franco entered the room. He walked slowly towards Caterina and looked directly at her.

"Is everything to your satisfaction, Signora Nazzari? Can I bring you anything?"

"Yes, Franco. All is fine."

His covertly flirtatious gestures didn't escape Suzette. She was intrigued. She'd also noticed how Caterina's mood changed when he came close to her. With his smouldering good looks and his toned physique, he could easily have been a model on the front page of Vogue. The expert cut on his expensive suit fitted him perfectly, showing the toned muscles in his thighs and calves.

After he'd left the room, Suzette posed the question.

"Caterina, is Franco your chauffeur *and* your butler?"

Caterina paused for a few moments. Unashamedly, she gave her answer.

"Franco plays a multitude of roles in my life. He is my chauffeur, my butler, my confidante, my companion and my gigilo."

She watched the expression on her guest's

faces and grinned.

"Yes. He is all of those. When my husband died, I had to have something in my life to excite me. Franco had been a guest in my home on many occasions when my husband entertained some of his friends and colleagues. After my husband died, he would call regularly to pay his respects and after an impromptu dalliance, I engaged him to look after my every whim."

Her smile was taut across her perfectly made-up face. Suzette wondered if she had succumbed to the surgeon's knife.

"Franco has a good life here with me. He keeps me young. He excites me. That doesn't mean to say that I don't miss my husband. I do. What I missed most was the intimacy of a man and Franco provides me with that intimacy. I don't ask him any questions about his private life. That's his business. As long as he does his job; and I must say he does it extremely well, then I have nothing at all to complain about."

Her openness about her 'arrangement' with Franco amused Serge.

Suzette's intuition had been right. She wasn't that lonely! Except, perhaps, when Franco had his days off.

"Do you know something. In the village where your son lives and nearby villages, there are many centenarians who are still sexually active. It's as natural as breathing is for them. I also intend to live a long and fulfilling life and, if Franco is here to satisfy my needs and keep me young, then it's well worth the exorbitant allowance I pay him. There's not a finer way to spend my inheritance."

More than satisfied with Caterina's answer, Suzette propositioned Serge.

"Do you think we might also live to become centenarians?"

"I think there's a strong possibility, but we'll have to keep practicing more regularly to make sure that we do!"

Franco appeared again with the maid and the remnants of the lunch were removed. It was time for them to go.

On leaving, they said they'd keep in touch with Caterina, but Suzette didn't know if they would.

Alex had already been admitted inside the grounds and was waiting for them.

"Well, did you enjoy your visit?

"You tell him all about it, Serge. All I can say is that it was a very interesting experience."

In explicit detail, Serge delivered a running commentary on Caterina's palatial residence and the information she'd disclosed.

Alex wasn't surprised. It was a well-known fact that many older women enticed younger men into their beds.

"We now know one of the secrets to living a long life", declared Suzette.

"Hey, Mum. There's a great deal of truth in what she says. Our research indicates that some of those people who are still sexually active, are in their nineties and even older!"

"Well, it seems to work for Caterina."

"We've also discovered, from the numerous completed questionnaires, that there are low rates of heart disease. There's not that many cases of Alzheimer's disease either. Brain health is good in older people who live here."

"Do you think it's in the genes, Alex?"

"That's what we are trying find out, Mum. It could be. It could be that they only eat fresh foods. They eat vegetables which they grow in their own gardens and they eat rabbit, chicken and fish. They also include a lot of rosemary in their diet, which is thought to improve brain function. Olive oil is used in cooking and as a dressing on foods."

Serge thought about their own healthy eating habits; lots of vegetables and fish. He'd met some of the locals when he'd taken strolls around the village and drank beer with them in the bars. Whilst he didn't speak much Italian, he could still join in with their discussions. Apart from the pronunciation and the syntax, most words were similar to his language.

"The children seem to have settled into the lifestyle here, Alex."

"Yes, Serge. The kids are multilingual now; more so than me! They're doing well at school and both have a love of reading. They don't watch that much television. They're always outdoors, playing sports with their friends. They're happy kids."

In two days' time, Suzette and Serge would return home. For Suzette, it would be difficult. It always was! She felt the same when she'd stayed with her daughter and grandchildren in England. The pull to stay with them had been strong.

"I'm going to make every single moment count within the next two days. I'm going to miss my grandchildren. I'm going to miss Annie and our conversations. I'm going to miss you too, son."

Alex knew only too well that she would.

"I'll miss you too, Mum."

CHAPTER FORTY NINE

Since returning home from their visit to Sardinia, Suzette reflected often on how much she missed her children and her grandchildren. She vowed to visit them more often or to invite them over to France; although they knew they didn't need an invite. They could come any time. She also knew that they had their own lives to live. Nevertheless, she felt that she would have liked a lot more time with them. The memory of Albert and Clio tugging at her skirt, begging her to stay, haunted her. She heard their voices in her sleeping dreams and in her daydreams – *"Grandmama, please stay. Don't leave us. We love you. Don't go."*

Serge had witnessed the drastic change in her temperament. Each morning, with a packed lunch and her writing materials, she'd go to the clearing and she'd stay there until early evening, gathering her thoughts and meditating.

One particular morning, after traversing the labyrinth, she sat in the summer house and picked up her pen to write.

On the blank piece of paper she wrote, *'Why do I feel this way?'*

She penned her answer.

'You feel this way because you have spent time with both of your children and their families and you miss them. It's natural to miss them. You taught them how to be independent and strive to achieve. They've experienced success and they are happy. You're proud of their achievements.'

Nostalgia sat down beside her and tenderly encouraged her to keep her pen moving.

'I know, but I wish they were small again and I could hold them in my arms and cuddle them; whisper sweet nothings in their ears and sing to them like I used to do.'

She put down her pen. She was usually so positive about her life and yet, over the last few weeks, she felt that she'd lost out on seeing all of her grandchildren grow up.

Her inner voice spoke gently to her.

"Come on, Suzette. Think about it. What is the purpose for feeling the way you do?"

Suzette thought for a while before answering herself. She knew that human oscillation, ever-present in her daily life, had unexpectedly challenged her emotions, upset her equilibrium and given her something to think about.

"I think the purpose is to make me realise how fortunate I am; that my beloved husband, my cherished children and my grandchildren are all happy and healthy. I'm so thankful for my life here and my ability to live the life I want to live. I'm grateful that Serge and I are together and that we have commonalities which we share. I love him dearly."

"Go back now to the house. Serge is very concerned about you. Spend some time with him. Have some lunch and talk to him about how you're feeling."

Gathering up her belongings, she wandered back and went to Serge's studio. He was sat at his workbench, sketching several images. His designs were strewn all over the bench and some were scattered on the floor.

As soon as he saw her, he rose from his chair and walked towards her.

"Hello there. Are you okay?"

She nodded and snuggled comfortably into the expanse of his warm, strong body.

"I'm sorry for my low mood, darling. I've felt so very miserable since my return."

He held her close. He'd sensed her low

mood on the return flight from Sardinia.

"Let's go and eat and we can talk about it."

Hands intertwined, they walked back to the house and went inside to prepare some lunch.

Suzette prepared a Caesar salad and set the table on the kitchen terrace, whilst Serge cut tofu into equal squares and coated them in cornstarch and chilli powder, before pan-frying them until they were crispy.

Over lunch, they discussed Suzette's recent mood and Serge's sketches.

"Let's go out for the day tomorrow, Suzette. Where would you like to go?"

Suzette watched her handsome husband as he poured more wine into her glass and she smiled at his natural thoughtfulness.

"Let's drive over to Pezenas. The market's on tomorrow. If we get there early, we'll be able to find a parking space by the palm trees."

"Good idea, Suzette. We haven't been there for a while. If we leave about 7.45, it'll only take us about an hour to get there."

After eating, Serge returned to his studio and Suzette, feeling much better, set about tidying the house. More motivated than she was earlier, she spent the afternoon scrubbing floors, rearranging furniture, and hand-washing some clothes. Sifting through her wardrobe, she packed several items of clothing, jewellery and scarves, all of which she hadn't worn in years into two large bags.

She'd take them along to the charity shop, which had recently opened in Lezignan, next week.

After dinner, they nestled together on the large sofa, watching the slivers of moonlight cast their shadows across the dimly-lit room.

In his arms, she knew that he understood her. He'd been holding space for her for the past few days to allow her to nurture her spirit and move through her vulnerabilities in her own way.

"I'm glad you're feeling better, darling."

"I am, Serge. The fog is beginning to lift."

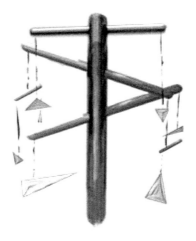

CHAPTER FIFTY

There was an extraordinary ambience about the intriguing, historic town. The ancient, stone buildings and artisan market in Pezenas held an habitual fascination for the regular visitors and the annual holidaymakers who frequented its cobbled streets and alleyways.

After breakfasting early, they drove along the near empty roads towards Pezenas. They knew it was imperative that they arrived early to secure a parking space; otherwise it would be a waste of time trying to locate one.

Serge locked the van door and joined

Suzette, who was waiting under the large expanse of palm trees, which took pride of place in the town centre.

The bustling Saturday market atmosphere drew them into the rows of market stalls, filled with fresh meats, cheeses and fresh vegetables. There were stalls selling fresh fish and seafood. Other stallholders sold a variety of dried fruits, honey and olives. Biscuit makers, chocolatiers and nougat makers generously offered mouth-watering samples to prospective buyers, in the hope of selling them their wares.

After tasting the chocolates and the nougat, Suzette didn't hesitate to buy a selection. Her sweet tooth had got the better of her and she, willingly, handed over her money in exchange for the delicious confectionery; speculating whether it would make it back to Lezignan, or if it would be eaten before they even arrived home.

Serge bought some tapenade, a variety of local cheeses and fish. He carefully arranged the foodstuffs into the cool box, before returning them to the van. He didn't want to carry them around with him.

The outstanding 16th and 17th century architecture dominated the entire town. With every corner they turned, the resplendent buildings raised their curiosity.

Ambling along, they passed several, French artists who were displaying their art. Some were using charcoal to sketch line-drawings of children and holidaymakers. Other artists chatted away to prospective buyers, explaining their distinctive techniques.

These paved, pedestrianised streets lined with ateliers and craft workshops were of particular interest to Suzette and Serge. Artistic vitality penetrated and overflowed into every space within the esteemed Ville et Métiers d'Art, Pezenas.

On entering the former 16th century, Consular Palace, which was the home for the Maison des Motiers d'Art exhibition hall, they could see a multitude of artists displaying individual and limited edition pieces of artwork.

Serge stopped at a stall where a young artist was painting. He initiated a conversation and was interested to hear that the young man lived near them in the village of Homps.

Suzette politely interrupted their animated conversation.

"Pardon Serge. I'm just going over towards the jewellery quarter. I want to see if I can find some unusual pieces."

"Ok. I'll wait here for you."

Suzette made her way over to a stall where a middle-aged woman was crafting. She watched as the woman adeptly threaded several amethyst and emerald tumble-stones, of different sizes, onto a lengthy piece of cord; using a knotting technique to hold them into place.

"Can I ask you what you're making?"

"I am just threading a length of crystals first. Then I'll decide later, whether to make a necklace or a bracelet, or maybe both", she replied.

Suzette was fascinated with the vast array of unique crystals which were randomly presented on a large piece of black velvet. The stunning colours and the uneven shapes, sizes and textures of the stones were captivating.

"I love those colours that you're using. Could you make a necklace and a bracelet for me please out of what you are working on?"

The artist handed over the work-in-progress to Suzette.

"These particular amethysts are from Siberia. Take a close look at the transparency and the deep richness of the purple. You'll see that they are of an excellent quality. The emeralds were shipped from Columbia. I don't have that many left."

Suzette touched the smoothness of the stones and inspected each one. The intense vividness of the emeralds were so powerful that she could feel their soothing energy having an immediate effect on her heart chakra.

The uneven amethyst crystals evoked a similar tranquil sensation when she touched them. Her spirit was lifting and bringing her back into balance.

"Yes. These crystals are for me."

"If you have a look around the hall and come back in an hour or so, I'll have your jewellery ready for you."

Thanking the artist, Suzette returned to find Serge, deep in conversation with the young man, who was still sculpting as he spoke.

"Hello darling. Did you buy anything?"

"Yes. The artist is completing it for me now. She asked if I'd return later."

Bidding farewell to his newly-found friend, he grasped Suzette's hand and they navigated their way through the market stalls, until they found the entrance.

Turning left, they located a restaurant which was situated within an open-air courtyard. Luckily, there was one free table. The atmosphere was vibrant as the attentive waiters quickly served generous helpings of food to hungry diners.

Whilst deciding on what to eat, the waiter offered them several small dishes of tapenades and chunks of home-made, rustic bread.

Serge ordered a cheese and asparagus quiche with a tomato and mozzarella salad.

Suzette chose the spicy, crusted tuna with a roasted nut salad.

During lunch they discussed the artists they'd met. Serge observed that Suzette's disposition was lighter, as she eagerly declared her desire to design new pieces of art. The artisan ambiance had fed her creativity.

"I can see that Pezenas has revitalised you, Suzette."

"It has, Serge. I feel more in balance today.

After eating a generous helping of home-made dessert, consisting of peanut butter ice-cream drizzled with a raspberry coulis, they paid the bill and rushed back to the exhibition hall.

The jeweller had already begun packing away her wares. The market closed at 2.00pm and it was already 1.50 pm.

After receiving payment, the jeweller carefully wrapped Suzette's purchase in white, tissue paper and placed it in a paper bag emblazoned with a logo advertising her brand.

The market place was emptying. They knew it would be difficult to even attempt to leave Pezenas at this time. The traffic would be so congested that it would mean them sitting in endless queues in the early afternoon heat.

They found a small café within a narrow street, and sat outside, sipping glasses of fresh lemonade topped with sprigs of mint.

Once the crowds had dispersed they walked back towards the van and, with clear roads ahead of them, they soon arrived home.

As they unloaded the van, the bags containing the chocolate and nougat were empty!

Later that evening, Suzette had changed her clothes to eat dinner. The crystal necklace and bracelet complimented the lime-green, shift dress that she wore. Her mind, no longer troubled, was sharper. Her recent adverse period of uncertainty had left her and she was now feeling at peace with herself.

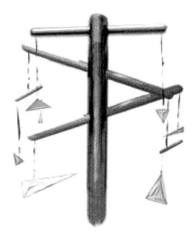

CHAPTER FIFTY ONE

The airport at Carcassonne was less bustling than it usually was. Parking the van had been relatively easy. Most of the summer-season holidaymakers had gone home.

Sarah didn't want to return home to England. She'd become very close to Hugo whilst she'd been in France. There had been times when she'd been frustrated with his peculiar behaviour and childish moods. The way in which he became exasperated when he couldn't verbally express his opinions, had been challenging for Sarah.

Deciphering whether it was part of his

autism, or whether it was because he was still grieving for his mother was also difficult. Trying to combat the silent episodes, had caused Sarah to wonder if her newly-found relationship was going to work.

In the week that Suzette and Serge were away, she'd also learnt that listening, really listening, to Hugo was important. She'd grasped that routine was critical for Hugo's wellbeing and, after a period of resistance, she'd fitted into that routine. Doing so had revealed different aspects of his personality; aspects that she liked!

Hugo had needed to escape from Sarah on a few occasions. Being with her exhausted him and he felt smothered by her good intentions of help.

He needed alone-time to think; to think about his feelings for her. He was falling in love with her and he didn't know what to do or to say. They'd already held hands and kissed; properly kissed! They'd also caressed each other and, when he felt her body against his, he wanted to have sex with her. He hadn't known whether he should tell her or whether he should be patient and see if it happened. Reading her body language was also difficult. He didn't know if she would want to have sex with him. He didn't know if she would want to commit to a relationship with him; if she would misunderstand his level of commitment to her and how his autism presented itself in ways which were alien to her.

He'd waited and the evening before Sarah

was due to leave, Hugo had plucked up the courage to speak with Sarah about having sex. His inability to lie about his feelings and his natural desire for her was so intense that he couldn't wait any longer.

Sarah had known that she felt the same way about him. She'd grown to love him in the short amount of time that she'd known him. It felt right.

Having sex with Hugo had not only sealed their relationship, it had made it all the more difficult for her to leave him. She knew that being with Hugo would demand compromises, for both of them. Adjustments would have to be made and, by just anticipating those changes, it caused her to feel apprehensive of what was ahead of her.

They'd both have to respect the validity of each other's perception on things. If Sarah could fathom his complexities and he could understand her needs, then their relationship could be just as successful, if not more successful, as anyone else's relationships; regardless of societal expectations!

To look at Hugo's external appearance, he was an exceptionally handsome young man. A man of high intelligence. His autism was not clearly visible until he was with people who were non-autistic. His eccentricity would then be deemed, by some people, as being unacceptable and lacking in social skills.

She thought of how any relationship could be fraught with difficulties. Getting to know each other and living with each other's ways were part of cultivating any relationship. She questioned how some people could be so derogatory about others' lives. Let them get on with their own lives! What right does any person have to judge how someone else lives?

When alone, Hugo and Sarah had discussed, in depth, the many world crises and the significance and purpose of human existence. She'd openly admitted to him that she hadn't comprehended all of what he'd eventually articulated; the language he used and his advanced intelligence, was far beyond her understanding.

She had fallen in love with his genuine concern for helping people and the damaging effect on the environment, his resolute fixations when striving to achieve his personal goals, his ever-so-handsome features and toned physique and, undeniably, his extended level of intellect. She'd fallen in love with the total package!

Serge and Suzette had strolled over to the other side of the car park, to allow them some time together. They were both concerned about Hugo's ability to deal with Sarah's departure.

After a lengthy affectionate embrace, Hugo left her after she'd handed in her luggage at the departure desk. As the sliding doors opened, he ran over to her and kissed her passionately.

"Come back to me Sarah. Don't leave me. I love you."

"I'll be back, Hugo. I love you too. I

promise you."

With tears clouding her vision, she turned and without looking back, she walked away from him. She just couldn't bear to see his woeful expression.

She knew, however, that she'd return soon: very soon!

CHAPTER FIFTY TWO

Once Sarah had returned home, Hugo had isolated himself. He'd already moved back into his home, before Serge and Suzette went to Sardinia; so it made it easier for him to become reclusive.

It took several attempts of coaxing before he would join the Coutures for meals and outings.

Serge had fabricated an excuse, saying that he needed help with chores in the orchard and other tasks in the studio. Hugo had agreed to help.

Serge even persuaded Hugo to learn how to drive.

Excited by the prospect, he'd applied for a

driving licence and Serge had arranged lessons with a local driving school.

Serge was certain that Hugo would fixate on the theory side of the driving test and grasp the fundamentals of driving in no time. It was a constructive distraction for him until the time when Sarah returned.

The application for his driving licence had been processed quickly and Hugo immediately decided to take an intensive driving course, where he would learn how to drive in a week.

He was determined to be driving by the time Sarah arrived.

The driving instructor was impressed with the speed in which he learnt to drive and especially with the exact recall of the answers to his theory questions. They were 'text-book answers'!

He arranged for him to take his driving test the following week and the examiner was equally impressed with his skills. He passed him, first time. He'd never passed anyone who had only been learning to drive for a few weeks before!

Serge and Hugo had spent many hours in car showrooms. After several days, Hugo decided to buy a Citroën C4. It wasn't a new car, but it did have a good service history and he collected it the following day.

With Serge's guidance, they'd arranged the car insurance and Hugo was driving Serge and Suzette around Lezignan and the wider locality, to get more practice for when Sarah arrived. He wanted to   surprise her, by collecting her from the airport and had made no mention of his achievement in his daily telephone calls to her.

****

In England, Sarah had been sorting out her affairs. She'd paid three month's advance rent on the premises in the health centre; in compliance with the terms of releasing herself from her contract.

She'd spoken to her mother about her plans to return to France, who wasn't very happy with the situation.   She'd told her to be realistic. Her list of questions had irritated Sarah.

"Do you know what you are getting yourself into?

"How many weeks have you known him?"

"However will you deal with his autism; his disability?

"Have you really thought this through? You've only known him for four weeks."

Hurt at her mother's unfeeling attitude and neurotypical ignorance towards Hugo's differences, she had strenuously defended him.

Sarah appreciated her mother's concern for her welfare and for her heart; but her heart told her that this was the right thing to do. She was willing to take the risk! She would focus on their commonalities, rather than their differences.

She would dispel the imbalanced societal myth that autistic people can't fall in love and be sexually intimate; and have a very successful relationship!

Her flights had been booked, her case packed and her mind made up. She was heading back to France to the man she'd fallen in love with and nothing, or no one, would stop her!

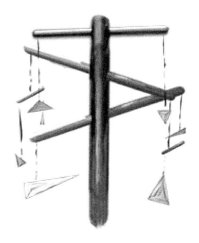

CHAPTER FIFTY THREE

He was waiting in the arrivals area when she came through the passport checking area.

They looked at each other and grinned.

He exhaled deeply. She'd finally come back to him.

He walked towards her, took her in his arms and held her close.

"Bonjour Sarah. I've missed you."

"I've missed you too, Hugo. An awful lot."

Hugo collected her luggage from the conveyor belt and, hand in hand, they walked over to the car park.

He couldn't take his eyes off her. She really was here with him.

"Where's Auntie Suze and Serge? How did you get here?"

He laughed and pointed to his car.

Whilst you were back in England I've been busy, learning how to drive. I've passed my test and bought a car.

"You haven't. Honestly?" she exclaimed.

He nodded.

"Yes. Honestly, Sarah. I took an intensive course and I passed my test within two weeks."

Amazed at his achievement, she shook her head and giggled.

"You didn't say anything about driving when we spoke on the telephone."

"No. I wanted to surprise you."

"Well, you have. Although, in future, I won't be surprised by anything you do!"

He placed her suitcase in the boot, opened the car door and gently eased her into the front seat, before closing the door.

His gentlemanly way made her feel special. His mother had taught him well. She'd noticed at other times, that he was very respectful of women.

Instead of taking the usual route home, He took a detour through the back roads and stopped at a secluded area alongside the Canal du Midi. He wanted to be alone with her. He wanted to kiss her. He wanted to hold her. He wanted more of her, but that would have to wait until later.

For now he just wanted to walk with her along the wide, tree-lined canal bank, watch the gentle ebb and flow of the languorous waterway, hold onto her hand and kiss her.

He'd willingly surrendered to the first throes of love, which were all-consuming. He wallowed in it as it flooded his brain and tantalised his hormones. The high-vibrational sensation was nothing like he'd ever experienced.

Sarah also felt light-headed. She'd had a few relationships, but never once had she experienced anything like the longing and love she felt for Hugo.

His desire mounting, he kissed her over and over again.

Lost in their own love-struck world, they were oblivious to their surroundings and hadn't noticed a barge approaching them and were startled when the occupants shouted over to them and waved.

"Bonjour. Bonjour", they all shouted.

They flinched. Their silent moment of passion had been disturbed.

"Bonjour," Hugo and Sarah replied in unison.

This part of the country was very special. The warm climate, the clean fresh air, the magnificent countryside and the relaxed pace of life. Sarah was looking forward to immersing herself in the French way of living and starting a new chapter of her life with Hugo. She was also looking forward to learning more of the French language. Yes, she thought that the Languedoc region would suit her.

"Let's go home, Sarah. I've prepared us a meal and then we have lots of things to catch up on."

Sarah knew exactly what he meant, as he took her in his arms and kissed her passionately again; pressing himself against her before they got into the car.

She wondered whether they would eat before or later!

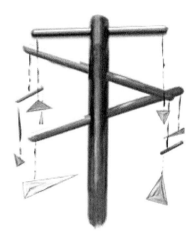

CHAPTER FIFTY FOUR

The test was positive. Sarah was pregnant; four week's pregnant! They were overjoyed. It hadn't come as a surprise to them. In fact, they'd half expected it; having made love at every opportune moment since Sarah's return. It was a natural bodily function for two people who were madly in love.

Excitedly, Hugo rang Serge and Suzette to see if they were at home. He nearly ended the call when Serge answered. He'd been in the garden.

"Hi, Père. Is it convenient for us to come over now?"

"Bonjour Hugo. Of course.

"Okay. We'll see you soon."

Unable to contain their excitement, they both climbed over the fence, and took a short cut onto the land next door.

Serge and Suzette were waiting for them on the kitchen terrace.

"Hello, you two. Is everything ok with you?" asked Suzette.

They both beamed and nodded.

Hugo couldn't get his words out quick enough to tell them.

"We, we want to share our news with you."

"What news would that be, Hugo? enquired Serge.

Anticipating the answer, Suzette looked at Sarah, raised her eyebrows and smiled.

"We're going to have a baby. Sarah is four week's pregnant."

Open-mouthed, Serge turned towards Suzette and blinked.

"Well, congratulations to you both. What wonderful news." You may not believe this, but Suzette was only saying just this morning, that she wouldn't be surprised if there were little ones running around here soon."

Sarah went over to Suzette and hugged her. Her aunt had always supported her when she was younger, when her mother had disagreed with her choices. She knew that she'd continue to do so throughout her pregnancy and beyond.

"Serge is right. I did say that. I somehow knew it would happen. It's a blessing for you both to have a child, especially when I can see how much you love each other."

"What do you think Mum will say, Auntie Suze?"

"Well, darling, I can imagine what she'll say, but it really doesn't matter. You can't live your life worrying what other people think about you, or what they'll say. It's your life. Live it. I'm thrilled for you both."

"I'm going to leave it until I'm three months and then I'll tell her. If she rings you, please don't mention it to her."

"I won't. It's your business, Sarah."

Suzette moved over to Hugo and embraced him. She loved him as if he was her own son. Over the past eighteen months she'd watched him mature on many different levels. During Nicole's illness he'd taken over the day-to-day running of the house, including the financial affairs. On a spiritual level, he was more self-aware and had learned to manage his autism-related moods through meditation and by channelling his energy into creative tasks. After Nicole's death, he'd allowed his own feelings of grief to erupt, instead of concealing them. It'd taken much effort on his part to make those changes, but he'd done it.

"I'm so proud of what you've achieved, Hugo. I'm so happy for you both."

"Thank you Suzette. I knew you'd be

pleased for us. Do you think Maman is around us?"

"I'm sure she is, Hugo. She'll be watching over you. Watch and listen. She'll come to you."

"She does, Suzette. She has. When Sarah was away, she came to me on several occasions. She said that I must do something with my life. I should help others who are on the autistic scale."

"So, have you decided what you'll do?"

"I've thought about it a lot lately. There's a school for autistic children in the next village. I've drove past it a few times and Sarah and I have spoken about it. I'm going to go over tomorrow and ask them if I can do some volunteering."

"That's an excellent idea, Hugo. You'll need a reference and some checks will need to made before they allow you to work there. We can give you a reference."

"Excellent idea, Serge reiterated. Now are you going to stay for lunch? Suzette's been baking all morning and we have lots of food which needs to be eaten."

"We'd love to eat with you", replied Hugo.

Hugo felt a cool breeze around the back of his neck and down his spine. He shivered. It seemed like his mother was also staying for lunch!

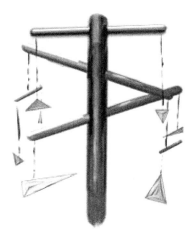

CHAPTER FIFTY FIVE

Hugo had telephoned the school and spoke briefly to the principal, who'd invited him for an informal interview.

He pressed the bell at the school entrance to announce his arrival and the principal came to the gate to welcome him.

Within her office, they spoke in length about Hugo's experiences and she gave him an overview of the school.

"Only twenty five pupils attend here. All are unique in that no two people present in the same way. We respect everyone's identity and try to develop their skills to help them to flourish and actively participate in society.   Lifelong learning is a major part of our curriculum. I collaborate with other autistic education establishments and this has enabled a strong network to be formed. We share resources, initiatives and sometimes we even share each other's employees.

She made copious notes as they spoke.

"I agree about uniqueness.   Difference being the key word. I also think that people with autism see the world in a completely different way. I don't necessarily consider myself to have a disability. I'm nineteen. I look after myself, I have a girlfriend and close friends who support me. I've recently passed my driving test. I embrace my difference. I know that I will always be autistic. I'm just me!"

The principal was more than impressed. Hugo was the type of person that she needed within the school to raise the self-esteem of the students and to motivate them.   He'd be an excellent role-model for the young people.

"I can see that you are quite high-functioning, Hugo?" she asked.

"As a young child, I was diagnosed as being high-functioning, but when my maman became ill and passed away, there were times when I was definitely functioning at a lower level. I fluctuate and react in different ways, according to how stressed I am. However, I have learned to manage my stress when it occurs. I suppose I react in the same way as any non-autistic person would react."

His contemporary approach to his own autism fascinated her. As the main agent of change within the school, she worked within the constraints of the national curriculum. However the innovative culture, which she'd developed and nurtured within the school had already witnessed increased success. Some of her ex-students had progressed into further education. With Hugo volunteering, there was now even more potential to introduce further changes.

"I would like to offer you a voluntary position. I need to speak with the local authority first and it's a requirement that we make the necessary safety checks before you can commence working with us. I will also need a reference."

"I can provide you with a reference."

Numerous concepts flooded her mind. Hugo's qualifications were excellent already, but she would professionally develop him further, if that was his choice.

She continued to make further notes before escorting Hugo off the premises, promising to call him two days later. As an autist, she knew he would respect being given an exact time.

"I will call you at two thirty on Wednesday, Hugo. Thank you for coming to see me today. You have enlightened me with your perceptive views."

Driving home, a voice whispered in his ear.

"Well done, Hugo. This is what you are meant to do. This is your birth mission."

"Thank you. I will do my best."

She knew he would be excellent in the role and do his utmost to help others.

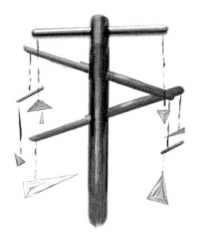

CHAPTER FIFTY SIX

At precisely 2.30pm on Wednesday afternoon, the principal called.

"Bonjour Hugo."

"Bonjour Madame Moreau."

"I'm pleased to inform you that I'm able to offer you a volunteering position within our school. It will be for three half-days initially. Does that suit you?"

"Merci, Madame. It does suit me."

"Would you like to commence working with us on Monday?"

Unable to contain his excitement, he had

some difficulty with pronouncing his words.

"M m m Monday? Yes. Monday is a good day for me. "

"I'll meet you at the school entrance at 9.30. It will give the students time to settle in before I introduce you to them."

"I'm really looking forward to it, Madame Moreau."

"Me too, Hugo."

After ending the call, he went into the kitchen, where Sarah was waiting to hear his news.

"Madame Moreau wants to me to start on Monday for three half-days a week. It's great news, isn't it?"

She pulled him towards her and held him tightly.

"It's fantastic news, Hugo. I'm so pleased for you."

Together they strolled along the lane, chatting animatedly, before turning into Villa d'Couture Atelier. He couldn't wait to tell them his news.

Suzette and Serge were busy pruning some shrubs when they heard footsteps on the pebbled driveway.

"Père. Suzette. I've been offered the job. I'm so excited. I start on Monday morning."

"Oh! Hugo. That's excellent news. We're so pleased for you. The job will suit your skills", Serge extolled.

"Most definitely, Suzette echoed his praise.

Let's go inside and talk about it."

Over peppermint tea and almond biscuits, they discussed Hugo's new job. He didn't really know that much about what he'd be doing. Madame Moreau would enlighten him further on Monday. All that he knew was that his gut feeling was telling him that it was the right thing for him to do; just like his maman had been previously telling him in his dreams.

Everything seemed to be falling into place. A few months ago he was in a very dark place. Now, his life had turned around. He had a beautiful woman in his life. He was going to be a father. He had acquired a job.

New pages of his life were being written!

CHAPTER FIFTY SEVEN

In the months that followed, Hugo's understanding and first-hand experience of autism served him well in his new job. He worked on several projects with the teenagers, assisting the teachers with many activities.

He was somewhat anxious when he first went into the school. In fact, he was totally exhausted after the first morning. Being with so many other people had reminded him of his time at school when he'd wanted to run away. He recalled how he'd felt and empathised with the young boys and girls who were there.

A stranger to begin with, he soon became a fixture, developing strong bonds with the students. They missed him not being there on his days off. Interpreting his own experiences and recognition of his own autism had instilled a newly-found confidence in the students and they were now open to taking risks that would improve their lives.

One student persistently challenged him.

"How can you be so positive about your life, when people judge you because of your autism?"

Hugo had calmly replied.

"They are ignorant about our differences in as much as we are ignorant about theirs. We must live our lives to the best of our abilities. We owe it to ourselves to strive for what we want. No one else can do it for us. Only we can do it."

The student wouldn't give up. He continued to grumble.

"But it's so difficult for me, Hugo. I can't do lots of things."

"Difficulties are gifts which are given to us to enable us to grow spiritually. Overcoming them is achievable, if you are just willing to try."

"I don't know if I want to. It's too difficult", came the reply.

"If anything was easy, then it wouldn't be worth doing, would it? Think about it."

The student had walked away, still disgruntled.

Whilst working at the school, Hugo had been invited to join an advisory committee where he was asked to help with diagnostic procedures. He was also instrumental in the setting up of an enterprise group where the teenagers produced and sold their goods.

Sarah's pregnancy was progressing well, with no difficulties. She'd also acquired some business premises near Olonzac, where she'd been working for two days a week.

As well as his job, Hugo had spent a great amount of time in his garden and at the labyrinth. He wanted to make sure the garden was kept to his maman's standard. That was what she would have liked! It was his commemoration to her life.

His habitual, daily visits to the labyrinth kept him focused. It fed his soul. It was his alone-time.

His part-time job was just enough for him. He wanted to spend time with Sarah and he was also studying for a teaching assistant's qualification, which he was determined to complete well before his deadline.

After a laborious duration of scrutinising and completing endless reams of paperwork, Hugo had succeeded in changing his surname to Couture. It was a difficult procedure, but a procedure that he'd been intent on finalising. It was something he'd promised himself. He'd wanted to take on Serge's name, ever since Serge had adopted a fatherly role before and after his maman had died. He loved him and respected him.

Whilst there had been several tense

moments in Hugo and Sarah's relationship, there had also been many ecstatic moments. They were very happy in each other's company. They'd agreed to disagree on some things. They'd even written their own manifesto, which included things what they both needed from their personal relationship.

When Hugo's fixations became too much for Sarah, he'd respect her request to cease talking about them. He understood that she didn't want to continually hear about his obsessions.

They'd also devised their own colour coding model for listing tasks. Red for urgent, green for not so urgent and yellow for no timescale.

When Hugo was fixated on something, nothing else mattered.

They completed some of their shopping on line and ate fresh fruit and vegetables from their own garden; although Sarah loved to pick up some bargains at the local markets with her Auntie Suze.

Sarah had learned to 'read' Hugo. She knew most of his foibles. Someone had once advised her that she needed to learn how to tolerate him. How rude of them. The word 'tolerate' didn't feature in her vocabulary. Tolerate meant 'putting up with' and she didn't put up with Hugo's behaviour. She loved him and everything that came with him.

One evening, after they'd eaten, the cramps started. Sarah thought it may be because she'd just eaten a large meal. Throughout her pregnancy she'd always felt hungry. She knew that she'd put on more weight than was advised, but Hugo's meals were so delicious, it would have been rude not to devour every morsel! That was her excuse anyhow!

It wasn't her time for giving birth. She had another two weeks to go; although she didn't really know what to expect.

Everything was ready for baby's arrival. Eve had kindly designed the nursery in neutral colours and she'd also re-designed the living room.

Suzette had also made several white layettes. They didn't know whether they were having a boy or a girl. They wanted it to be a surprise.

The pains seemed to get worse and Sarah took herself off to bed. She needed to lie down.

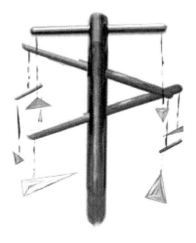

CHAPTER FIFTY EIGHT

Throughout the night, her discomfort worsened. Her unbearable, cramp-like pains were now coming every twenty minutes. She realised that she was in the early stages of labour.

She nudged Hugo.

"I really think I'm in labour, Hugo. The pains are more frequent now."

He'd read about the stages of labour and he began to question her.

"Are they just niggling pains or are you having contractions?"

At that moment the contractions returned.

They took her breath away. She didn't answer him.

"Sarah, are you ok? How many minutes in between each contraction?"

The pains ceased and she started to laugh.

"Hey, Doctor Hugo. When did you graduate as a midwife?"

Chortling, he continued to question her.

"Seriously, how many minutes. It's important, Sarah."

The concern on his face prompted her answer.

"I would estimate them to be about fifteen minutes now. The pain's in my stomach and my lower back. It's the worst pain ever, Hugo."

"Just try and do your breathing exercises."

She laughed again. She loved the way he was doing his best to help her. She also knew that with each pain, her precious baby was struggling on its way to being born; so she wasn't complaining.

"Arrghh! Arrghh! Hugo. That wasn't fifteen minutes. I think our baby's ready to be born."

Panicking, he rang Suzette.

"Suzette. Can you come quickly? I think the baby's coming. Well, I don't think; I know it's coming."

"Are you sure, Hugo? The baby's not due for another two weeks."

"I know Suzette, but Sarah's pains are coming every fifteen minutes or less, now. Can you come now. I don't know what to do."

"Of course, I'm on my way over. I'll be with as soon as I can."

Serge, hearing the conversation, had quickly dressed. Suzette threw a jumper over her head and stepped into her jeans.

As the van pulled up on Hugo's drive, he was waiting at the door for them.

"Quick. She's in agony. The pains are coming sooner now and she says they're getting stronger."

Suzette waited for the contractions to stop.

"Have you got your bag packed, Sarah? I think your baby will soon be here. We need to get you to the hospital."

"Yes. It's just over there. Can you pass me my dressing gown please? I don't want to deliver the baby here, or in the car. Let's go."

As she stepped out of the bed, the pains had returned. They were excruciating. She felt nauseous.

She managed to get into the car and reach the hospital just in time. Suzette had rang them on the way and the midwives were waiting for her at the entrance. She was transferred immediately into the delivery room and helped onto the hospital bed. She felt a sudden urge to push. Hugo held tightly onto her hand as the waves of pain washed over her. With one enormous push, the baby was born; a little boy with jet-black hair and a nose like Hugo's.

The midwife quickly checked the baby and

wrapped him in a white sheet before handing him to Sarah.

"You have a beautiful baby boy, Sarah. 4.76 kilos. He's a big one. Well done."

"Well done, Sarah", a voice whispered in her ear. She knew who it was!

The pains were soon forgotten as she held him in her arms.

Hugo kissed her and he kissed the baby's head.

"Sarah. He's so beautiful. Thank you for giving me a son. I love you."

"Hey, you had some involvement in this, too!"

Her tears were happy ones as she handed the baby to him. She wanted him to bond with his son.

Serge and Suzette were quickly ushered into the delivery room.

"Sarah! He's perfect. He's gorgeous. You're both very blessed", gushed Suzette.

Serge, totally mesmerised with the tiny bundle in front of him, congratulated them.

"A boy. How wonderful for you both. Have you thought of a name for him?"

"We have. We'll name our baby boy, Nico Serge Couture", Hugo proudly announced.

Serge gasped, then wept uncontrollably.

"Nico, after my maman and Serge Couture after you, my Père. Your new grandson will carry on your family name. Here, hold him."

Suzette glanced at Serge as Hugo placed the not-so-tiny baby gently into Serge's outstretched arms.

Nico's grand-père held him tightly to his chest and whispered in his ear.

"Hello little boy. We've all been waiting for you to arrive. Welcome to our family."

Coming soon

Read a brief preview of the third novel
in Susan's trilogy.

Hugo's Child

It was Nico's fifth birthday. He looked at the clock;
6.00am precisely. He always woke up at that time.

Later, in the afternoon after he'd attended
his pre-school, he would host a birthday party.
Only one school friend, Enzo, would be attending.
The other eight people attending the celebration
would be adults.

He'd been attending the Ecole Maternelle
school in Lezignan for four half-days since he was
three years old.

Even though, in France, the compulsory age
for children to commence school was six, his
mother had wanted him to mix with other children.
Recently, she'd heard on the news that the new
president was soon going to make it compulsory for
children to attend school at the age of three; in his
effort to reduce inequality in education. She'd
wondered whether the new education law would
bring about some resistance.

During several discussions with some
French mothers, she'd learnt that whilst they
wanted their children to have some form of pre-

schooling, they also sought to nurture a close relationship with them before they went to school on a full-time basis.

Nico didn't like going to school. It wasn't that he didn't like learning; he did! He loved to learn about numerous things, but he knew he was different from the others. They didn't want to play with him. They called him names. He just didn't 'fit in'.

Reading was just one of his many compulsions. His distinct bookishness had led him to acquire many fictional and non-fictional books, which he kept in librarian-order in a large bookcase in the corner of his bedroom. His writing skills had been compared with those of an eleven-year old and his mathematical skills were excellent.

Nico was articulate in French and English, with an extended vocabulary for his age. He'd spoken in coherent sentences when he was eight months old.

His father was French by birth and his mother was of English descent. Although his mother had a northern English accent, when Nico spoke English his accent was formal and somewhat pedantic. His linguistic oddity became the topic of conversation when people met him for the first time.

Nico didn't particularly like being with children of his own age. He much preferred the company of his adult relations and friends. He felt comfortable just by being around them.

At the grand age of three, he had been placed in front of a piano and had stunned his parents with his ability to play. Since being a baby, he had listened to all genres of music, including classical concertos. With much encouragement from his grandfather, he'd learnt to replicate some of the famous classical composers and he'd practice repeatedly until he'd perfected the complicated melodies.

When singing songs, he was word-perfect; his rote memory being excellent. If others sang the words incorrectly, he'd soon correct them.

For most of the time, Nico was happy to be in his own company; especially when he was busy acquiring knowledge about a range of, what would appear to others to be, monotonous subjects.

He wasn't appreciative of any interruptions when he was concentrating. Neither did Nico welcome any change to his daily routine. Comparable to other children of his age range, he was inclined to have tantrums.

Bordering on genius, Nico had been diagnosed as being a high-functioning autist. There was always the possibility that he'd be autistic.

The diagnosis had come as no surprise to his father, who was also a high-functioning autist!

About the author

Susan Higgins is a semi-retired teacher of English, a fictional/technical author and an experienced facilitator of change.

As an author of fiction, her writing is inspired by the Languedoc region of France and her perpetual passion for her own self-development and the advancement of others; on both an academic and a spiritual level.

Over the past ten years, she has designed and delivered creative writing courses. She has also written and delivered many self-development programmes.

As an author of non-fiction, her written matter includes technical procedures and media journals for various reputable organisations.

The author invites you to leave book reviews on www. amazon.co.uk

Oscillate is the second novel in Susan's trilogy; the first one being The English Recluse, which is about a woman whose innate reasoning encourages her to confidently follow her spiritual path.